UNINVITED GUEST, UNEXPECTED GIFTS

A JOURNEY THROUGH BREAST CANCER

TJITZE DE JONG

Also by Tjitze de Jong

Pizza's of Boeremoes
Koperative Utjowerij, Bolsward, The Netherlands, 1988

Cancer, a healer's perspective (Insights, stories and messages of hope)
amazon.com amazon.co.uk, 2011

Love or Lust I, *according to Charlotte*
amazon.com amazon.co.uk, 2011

Love or Lust II, *according to Fergus*
amazon.com amazon.co.uk, 2011

Love or Lust III, *according to Rhanna*
amazon.com amazon.co.uk, 2011

The Wife of Macbeth
amazon.com amazon.co.uk, 2020

To be published:
Energetic Cellular Healing and Cancer (Treating the emotional imbalances at the root of disease)
Inner Tradition, USA, expected February 2021

Tjitze de Jong was born in The Netherlands and now lives on the banks of River Findhorn, Scotland. In the 1980s he published a novel (Pizza's of Boeremoes), short stories, book reviews, poetry and was co-editor of magazines 'Hjir' and 'De Harpe'. Twice he won short story awards and all this in his native Frisian language. Some two decades after moving to Scotland he began writing in English.

During the last 25 years he has developed a global reputation as healer and founded Tjitze's Energetic Cellular Healing School in 2007.

Published in 2020 by

Tjitze de Jong amazon.com and amazon.co.uk

ISBN: 978-1-5272-7371-9

THANK YOU .....

..... first and foremost to the thousands of clients who allowed me to work with them during these last 25 years. Your inner drive and dedication to your health and well-being shall always remain a source of inspiration to me.

..... Kate for being so generous with your time and your impeccable knowledge of the English language.

..... Niki and Ianto for allowing me to use your expertise and computer skills in order to make a rough manuscript into a novel ready for publication.

Uninvited Guest, Unexpected Gifts

CHAPTER ONE

When she dried her left upper arm, the back of her hand stroked the outside of her breast, coincidentally. Of course, coincidentally. Or was it? Or was the back of the hand searching for confirmation of what the fingertips, all ten of them, had traced and retraced hundreds, if not thousands of times these last couple of days?

The discovery of the fingertips' touch had been pushed to the back of her mind, way back. "Pushed" was too weak a verb. The findings had been crushed, jarred, bulldozed, hammered into the furthest recesses of the mind, where only the mind itself had access. And that same mind knew its privilege of being sole visitor, if not intruder. And that same mind directed the fingertips hundreds, if not thousands of times to that same outside of that same left breast. Those very same fingertips kept sending those very same messages of confirmation to that very same mind of what that very same mind itself refused to accept, comprehend and acknowledge as truth. Her inner battle raged and gave no respite whatsoever.

If she would succumb and acknowledge the truth, it might well shatter a day to day sense of secure reality into a maelstrom of fear. Therefore, she kept tricking herself with a vague perception, with self-deception and with procrastination.

Procrastination.

She found it a yakkie word: procrastination. It was made up of so many syllables, cut off into sharply jarring pronunciation.

She'd learned the word's full impact during a kind of sinister board game she'd played the previous month when there had not yet been ..... The ten fingertips obeyed the mind and retraced yet again.

According to the guy who'd run the show, this very game managed to scratch ones blood away from underneath ones nails by dragging dormant fears, patterns, insecurities and the like into conscious awareness. It could turn out to be a somewhat painful process and not for the faint hearted. He had stressed these points several times and addressed the four playing women as bravehearts during the introductory half hour of the weekend workshop. No doubt he had intended these remarks as a compliment to the quartet's courage.

At some point towards the end of the first afternoon she had received a so-called Setback Card, which read:

"You are setback by your procrastination on your present level. Take 2 pains."

The two added pain tokens (small dark blue squares of card with a white tear drop) had dumped her into depression. Earlier she'd already received two pain tokens, apparently because of some faulty intuition, whatever that meant. Twice a dice roll had told her to flip a coin and the gold coloured piece had landed with the tear drop showing both times. A totality of four pain tokens meant depression, according to the extensive rule book. All in all it had taken her three turns, i.e. until the middle of the second day, the Sunday, to dispose of the pains.

The other three women had been able to complete several

moves successfully, gained pleasant Insight Cards and piles of positive Awareness Tokens, had moved from Physical through Emotional and Mental Level onto the Spiritual Level. They had supported each other and had laughed loads.

And she herself? She'd been stuck. Stuck forever it seemed on that darned Physical Level, the level for beginners. Throughout almost the entire weekend she had had to cry. Not to cry, hadn't been an option, especially with the kind of deeply digging questions the guy had, rather rudely, fired in her direction. She'd hated it and she'd hated him for it.

He had smiled and nodded and had, infuriatingly, made forever the right sounds, the right remarks and had asked the right questions with a series of facial expressions, indicating his compassion, his understanding and his empathy. Also, he had supplied her with an endless stream of tissues.

That day it had taken all her effort not to burst into a tantrum and sweep board and cards and tokens and dice off the round table. When a Miracle move from one of the three other women had lifted all pains in the game, including her own depression, she had sobbed uncontrollably. Inwardly relieved, she had bluntly refused to answer any further questions and handing over tissues had remained the guy's only privilege, however shatteringly humiliating it felt. She had personified the cry baby of the group. She, who never shed a tear, at least not in company. And then, unexpectedly, she had exposed herself to such a two day marathon of tearful mess.

During the two hour return train journey and later on at home, reflections had made her realise how often she did procrastinate. She had always done that for as long as she could remember and most likely she wouldn't ever be able to break the habit.

During years gone by, two men had proposed to her. Her "yes" had been postponed and her decision procrastinated. Each of the two boyfriends' patience had been severely tested and they had failed. Both times, when the men broke off the relationship, she had plunged head over heels into depression.

9

She found herself in one now. In a depression that was, not in a relationship. That's why she had taken the risk to play that wretched game. A relationship, that's what she was after, rather yesterday than tomorrow.

The game weekend had failed to bring her any further. That pattern of procrastination had been the only seemingly significant revelation. Okay, maybe it was not a totally new insight, for frequently she had become annoyed with herself, when she didn't pick up the courage to take a risk and break a habit of a lifetime. Indecisiveness had often left her in limbo and intensified a stuckness, which easily deepened into feeling hopelessly depressed. All of that was nothing new, but, now it had a name.

So what? Did the fact that she could put a name to it, make it any easier to stop the habit? That chap hadn't handed her any tools. Were there any? Was there anything she needed to change or could change? If so, what and how could she do it? It had not been for want of trying during that weekend, because the rubbish bin had practically overflowed with tissues, almost exclusively her tissues filled with her tears and her snot.

And all of that was nigh on a fortnight prior to her fingertips tracing a slight hardening of tissue and well a very different type of tissue. Not the kind of tissue she could throw in the bin and be done with.

This tissue was inside of her. It grew inside of her at her expense and had decided to become part of her against her will. At least that's what her fingertips wanted the mind to believe, even if the latter bluntly refused to take it on board. Did that spot of hardness grow or was it just the mind playing tricks? Was it there in the first place? Then again, the back of the hand had, today, when drying herself after showering, also registered that very same hardening of tissue for the very first time. Had the back of the hand been brainwashed by a frightened mind to register the lump? Impossible, she mused, for the back of the hand contained no brain cells. Only the brain did. And then again, was the brain objective or had it already been brainwashed by itself into forcing her to believe the worst case scenario?

A cyst, an ordinary cyst created a similar feeling. Or, did it? What did a cyst feel like actually? What did the other kind of hardening feel like, the harmful kind, the scary kind? Was there a palpable difference between both and if so, how and what was the actual difference?

She didn't know enough about either of the two phenomena to draw any reliable conclusion. Normally, when she was unsure of anything, she asked google or wikipedia and always received some kind of answer. She didn't dare this time round. Exploring either possibility, drew both of them into the realms of reality. Also the worst one and that needed to be avoided at all cost.

Alternatively, she could phone a friend, but also this she didn't dare. Confiding in one of them, was going to make her own suspicions more concrete. Besides that, had any of them experience with such a delicate matter? Not as far as she knew. None seemed applicable. It was just as well that none of her friends seemed applicable. Otherwise she would have known and that would mean that one of them had at some point been confronted with ..... had at some point been confronted with the unmentionable.

Then again, after her mother's death most friends had left her. All of them, to be precise, which put her in a rather shameful, friendless position. Especially nowadays, when people's self images were intricately linked with the number of friends on Facebook or Twitter and the number of 'likes'.

Ringing NHS 24 was at least an anonymous service, hence less self exposing and humiliating. Still, ringing the NHS had the same effect of making a vague suspicion more concrete and that she didn't dare.

She didn't dare to take a step, to take any step, which might entail shifting suspicion into a more concrete reality.

She swallowed a sleeping tablet, drank a couple of glasses of red wine, rather large ones, but still, only two and went to bed. She pulled the covers over her head just a touch further than usual. Sleep was slow in approaching despite alcohol and drugs.

Uninvited Guest, Unexpected Gifts

CHAPTER TWO

Sleet splashed in thick clusters on the Velux windows, driven
by fierce north westerly gusts and sank, partly dissolving on
its way down, before it joined the three inches of slush, which
grew neither shrank at the bottom of the window panes. The
melting kept pace with the shower's intensity. Or, could
several uninterrupted hours of a wet and windy onslaught still
be called shower? The forecast had only mentioned passing
showery activity.

The slush filtered daylight into an insubstantial greyness.

Fluorescent strip lights seemed to glare stronger as a result
in the waiting room. Their shrill light shone over a desolate
scene of leaking umbrellas, sopping shoes, overcoats and hats
in various stages of soddenness. Not a single seat was
unoccupied and several people stood against a wall, dripping.

An occasional whisper breached the unwritten law of silence
in a herd of sheeplike humans driven together by fate into each

others forced company, trying to find commiseration in joint misery and failing. Many coughed or blew noses or both and forced their neighbours to make space for movement, where there barely was any.

Every so often a new arrival entered. Every so often somebody left, obeying the red, frantically moving letters of the notice board, announcing a name and a room number.

The people arriving and leaving kept pace with each other like the three inches of slush on the window panes and the waiting room remained full to capacity. The muddy puddles on the floor joined gradually into a shallow lake with seven doorsteps as dykes, preventing consultation rooms to become flooded.

All of these observations didn't do anything to lift her mood. She had felt miserable already when she awoke from a fitful sleep, when she'd prepared to leave the house, when she'd stood in the crammed tube and when she'd walked direction health centre. This is where she stood now, squashed in a corner and surrounded by the epitome of collective misery. In turn, she held her breath and sighed deeply, but then as inaudible as practically possible.

It took all of her thin courage to withstand the urge to flee and escape to nowhere in particular, but away, away from the desolate waiting room. She waited for her name to appear in bright red for all present to notice. Each new arrival and each new announcement thinned her courage further until a mere shred remained. Her courage was nothing but a thin, threadbare shred, frayed and on the verge of tearing.

Wind swept sleet.

Each dripping newcomer deepened the puddles and increased muddiness.

The one storage heater, tiny and scruffy, did not have the slightest impact on a chilled dampness.

Two conversing people entered and as on command all faces turned in their direction. The unanimous wave of judgements made the couple fall silent and join the masses in their complacency.

Nothing escaped her attention. Although, she tried to make sure that nobody would notice her watching. She didn't want to add to people's discomfort by intruding on them. Likewise, she didn't want to be intruded upon or draw attention onto herself. At the same time, she felt the desperate urge to move, preferably away from the gloominess, as far as possible and as soon as possible. As long as her name didn't appear on the screen, she couldn't move without entering the lime light and make all these heads and eyes turn in her direction together with all these judgements.

She felt trapped in that corner. She had cornered herself, well and truly and berated herself for voluntarily setting up her own trap and entering it with wide open eyes. Almost two months after her ten fingertips had traced the first hint of a distortion in her soft breast tissue, she'd finally decided to take the plunge. She had rung the local health centre, where she'd registered six years earlier, well over six months after moving to the area. All appointments for that day had been filled and she had been advised to ring again, next day at eight. Ringing back had slipped her mind that next day. At least that's how she'd tried to trick herself in believing, unsuccessfully. And she'd remembered again some two days later. Obviously, forgetting had been out of the question. She had refused and rebelled against her own inner authority. It hadn't been a matter of procrastination, but rebellion.

Her second attempt to book an appointment had had a similar result. Third time lucky, she'd told herself when she put the phone down. Well, this kind of luck was not worth crossing her fingers for, like the secretary had advised her to do both times she'd been refused. Had luck brought her one step further? Further indeed in the sense, that the earlier solitary misery had turned into a shared misery amid a bunch of utter strangers. Could that be called progress?

Cut off in contemplation, she missed her name appearing on the notice board, however aggressively it flashed in electronically induced impatience.

An urgent, computerised voice called her name and dragged her back to reality. She left her corner by pushing her way through wet coats and by stepping on toes. In front of the automatic doors she adjusted her coat, hat and scarf, clutched the handbag tightly under her left arm, opened the umbrella and battled her way back home against driving sleet. She wanted to get away from this dreadfully desolate place which could only increase her anxiety.

Uninvited Guest, Unexpected Gifts

CHAPTER THREE

Yet again her name appeared on the notice board. She rose, draped and hooked her coat, hat, scarf and umbrella over her right arm, made sure the handbag was secured in its usual place before she inhaled deeply and knocked on the door of consultation room number six.

Christmas had been and gone. New Years Eve and New Year's Day ditto. Her main new year's resolution had been to get the initial GP visit over and done with at the earliest opportunity.

That was today, the third of January, just over four weeks after many rivers had burst their banks, whilst storms had played havoc with traffic, trees, coastal regions and a string of towns and villages. Especially Wales and the south west had suffered badly, according to the BBC, whilst they showed the annual footage of flooded fields and housing estates and the emotional devastation of families unable to celebrate the festive season under their own roof.

Their fate, forced upon them by a natural disaster, had made her aware of her own good fortune. Not falling victim to such exceptional weather induced circumstances had motivated her to take fate in her own hands, finally. This New Year's resolution, she was in the process of obeying, was the result.

A female voice bade her come in.

She pressed the door handle down and shivered. In a couple of months' time, she'd celebrate her thirty sixth birthday.

Fate had skipped two sixes. At the age of six, she'd fallen from the stairs and dislocated her left elbow and had to go to hospital three times, for plaster, for a check up and to have plaster removed. When twelve she had crashed with bicycle and all over a bridge at a downhill section, had ended up with severe concussion, a broken right wrist and had to go to hospital another three times. For the first two of these visits she had to be transported back and forth by ambulance. Then, when she was eighteen, an old lady in a red car had failed to give way and knocked her of her bicycle, resulting in a second concussion and three broken upper teeth. Serenaded by sirens and blue lights she'd been hospitalised for a week.

At twenty four she had expected disaster, but it didn't materialise and at thirty she'd remained slightly suspicious, but again nothing happened. Now, six times six, at least in several months' time, the pattern continued. An eerie set of coincidences, she thought, whilst standing outside the consultation room, still pressing the door handle down.

The female voice repeated the invitation with an added a hint of impatience.

Her allocated GP, whom she'd never met before, peered in her direction over silver rimmed glasses when the patient entered. She stroked her long, wavy chestnut hair behind one ear. The other side cascaded freely onto the desk, partly covering the arm.

Suddenly she was no longer an ordinary woman, but relegated into a patient. The doorstep, which had kept floods at bay the previous month, now functioned as a portal.

"On the one side, I'm an ordinary woman and on the other side, I'm a patient." she thought and made the decisive step over the threshold.

The piece of philosophy startled her. The surprise that her own brain was capable of inventing such aptness, was soon pushed aside by the notion, that something was expected of her. Something with which she barely had any experience. Something, which placed her in an unfamiliar role, an uncomfortable role of dependency. And so she stood, still holding onto the inside door handle. Was she in need of some kind of support? Was she clinging onto the final straw before changing into a patient with still the option of escape within reach as long as she held on to the handle? Releasing it, implied a further move towards the inevitable. She did though, ever so reluctantly. It was as if she had to pull her fingertips away, as if they were glued to the metallic surface with chewing gum, stretching, stretching, stretching before she managed to take the next step.

"Come and take a seat."

The doctor's head, slightly askance for her hair to remain locked behind the ear, jutted forward just a bit.

She sat down. The metallic frame of the chair bounced a bit, making a speedy exit easier if need be, she noticed. Her hands gripped the arms of the chair. She reminded herself of her New Year's resolution and remained seated.

"What can I do for you?"

The face opposite smiled and the voice sounded friendly.

That made it a bit easier to stay and not bounce off immediately. Her mind raced and tied all of her in knots, for she approached the moment when a truth was about to be revealed, the truth about her left breast, her precious left breast, What could she expect in the forthcoming weeks or months, if not years or decades when push came to shove and the doctor was to pronounce that dreaded diagnosis?

The other woman checked her watch and meant it obviously

as a gesture of pressure for the patient to get to the point.

"Well, I need you to look at my breast, my left breast. There's something hard growing and I'm afraid....."

"No problem. I'll do that for you. When did you first notice it?"

"About three months ago."

She said it with the thin voice of a little girl, who expects to be reprimanded. Her eyes avoided the doctor's eyes and busied themselves with trying to upside down decipher the writing on the collection of orange, yellow, green and pink post-its, neatly stuck along the left edge of the wide desk. The thin voice turned out to be justified, when she detected a sharp edge in the doctor's voice.

"Why did you leave it so long?"

"Don't know, really."

"And the growth has not previously been picked up by a mammogram? Or, have you not kept your regular appointments?"

"No."

"Why not? Such a scheduled service has been allocated to you as a preventative measure."

"I know. I'm sorry. I went once and didn't like it."

The doctor wrote something down and stopped looking at her patient.

"My guess is, you have examined your breast yourself? And if that's the case, have you examined it frequently?"

The patient nodded.

"Are you registering any change in size or texture?"

"It's growing."

"And the fact that it's growing made you decide to come and see me? How large would you say it is now?"

Her thumb and index finger indicated a couple of inches space.

"How big, would you say it was, when you first felt it?"

Her thumb and index finger moved closer together and together they saved her from having to speak. She didn't want to speak. The ever thinning voice she kept hearing didn't sound at all like her own, but a voice alienated from the rest of her as if programmed by some sort of external computer.

What she craved was, for the doctor to ask her to lie down, rock her into slumber and remove what needed removing and for her to awaken refreshed and leave the episode behind as a nasty dream without further consequences or responsibilities.

Instead the doctor had said something. Had it been a question? Had she been expected to answer?

"Sorry? I didn't get that."

"Are you all right?"

"Yes, I'm fine. Sorry, what was your question?"

"If you would like me to have a look. I will need to touch the area in question, but I shall be as discreet and quick as possible. It isn't painful normally, but if you feel any discomfort, please inform me. Are you OK with that?"

She nodded.

"Great, thank you, if you'd be so kind to remove the upper half of your clothing, so we can check the area of complaint. I would like to make you aware, that at this early stage I shall not be able to provide you with a full diagnostic report. If necessary, I shall refer you for a scan, which will give us a clearer indication of the state of affairs. Once that information has been made available, we can discuss our treatment plan, again, if necessary. But, let's not get ahead of ourselves. First things first. Thank you."

She had removed her blouse and bra. In preparation of what lay ahead, she had showered more thoroughly than normal that morning and had used plenty of deodorant. It proved a useless effort, because all the tension had made her sweat profusely and both pieces of clothing felt dampish to the touch. She had taken the opportunity, when the doctor was scribbling some more notes on her file, to lift her left arm and smell her armpit and was disgusted by the own BO. It was as if she visited her dentist after eating garlic without brushing her teeth. What

21

would she be thinking of her hygiene standards, she thought and her arms hugged her sides when the doctor approached.

"Which breast shows the symptom?"

"The left one."

"And where in the breast is the growth located?"

"On the outside."

With the hands moving came the question, whether she was OK with being examined.

Trying to protect the doctor from her armpits' perspiration and simultaneously shrugging her shoulders proved too awkward a movement to accomplish and the awkwardness tensed her entire body even further. She knew how she hated lying in the dentist chair, but this was due to be quite different. This doctor was not going to hurt her and there were not going to be any horrible noises or poking implements stuck inside her mouth. Still, she remained scared. Scared of the whole scenario: the interview, the doctor's judgements about her not attending a single mammogram for over a decade and about her waiting several months before making an appointment She remained scared of the prodding, of the doctor's findings and diagnosis and of the likely need for a scan. Her mind turned into a whirlwind of uncontrollable worries and when the other woman told her to relax, she felt berated even stronger and told herself to chill, which had the opposite effect.

The fingertips moved swiftly, all ten of them, although not her own fingertips this time.

The procedure felt so different from when she examined herself.

It was more intimate because somebody else's fingers fondled one of her most intimate body parts.

Her breasts had received the thumbs up from her boyfriends in the past. If only she could take a man's compliments about breasts serious. Each positive comment seemed an excuse to fiddle with them with any kind of compliment as justification and she, whose breasts they were, ultimately, had rarely ever had a say in the matter.

Also more intimate, because the person touching her, was female like herself. Having her breast fondled by another woman seemed more intrusive somehow. She was not lesbian, never had any inclination in that direction and refused to be stigmatised as such and as a result, she experienced each finger movement as an intrusion and shivered often.

"Are you cold? It wont be much longer."

"No, I'm fine, really."

The touch felt less intimate than that of a boyfriend, because the woman who fondled her breast had a profession and acted in that role. Her mind knew that and took solace in the knowledge. This time, the nipple was avoided at all cost, whereas each man had concentrated heavily on nipples, erecting it through stimulation in whatever shape or form. They had frequently been overriding her pain threshold and had made her gasp. Her noises had turned them on even more.

"Thank you. You've been most cooperative. Feel free to get dressed again."

She did, whilst the doctor wrote some notes during a minute when icy silence ruled.

The bigger half of her was dead curious and she wanted to blurt out the all important questions:

"And, tell me, please? Do I have cancer or don't I?"

Her smaller half was filled with a shivering trepidation and still wanted to do a runner before the doctor could open her mouth. That wish was called procrastination, she now knew. How could such a knowledge support her at such crucial moments? That weekend had all been nonsense. This, what the woman opposite her was going to reveal, that is what she had to face right now. This was real life.

As long as the doctor focused on her paperwork, she dared to look straight at her. It was a pretty woman who knew how to present herself with touches of make-up, with precisely applied eyeliner and lipstick and a perfectly natural touch of rouge.

No sooner did the pretty woman raise her head and renewed

the eye contact with her patient, then the latter averted her eyes.

"Well, I can state the obvious and confirm your own observation, that there is indeed a growth developing in your left breast. Whether it is malignant or not, I cannot say. I shall leave the diagnosis to the specialist. Therefore, I shall write the oncology department an e-mail, requesting them to schedule an appointment with yourself. They will get in touch with you as soon as possible."

"How long will that take?"

"It is impossible from my position to give you an exact date."

"But you must know whether it will be one week, or two, or a month?"

"Quite impossible for me to give you an exact indication about the length of time it'll take, normally several weeks."

"But, surely, scheduling an appointment doesn't take that long?"

"I'm awfully sorry, but it may. I regret that I can not be any clearer."

The non-committal vagueness made the doctor sound like a politician prior or during an election campaign. A hint was being given and the public had to content itself with this non-committal level of information. Nothing the wiser and tense as a result, she barely breathed. Normally she would not make a fuss, but in a desperate attempt to quench her fear, the question arose. Afterwards she would never ever have been able to say where the question had arisen from or where her bravery to ask had appeared from. It was the first time her mind thought that blasted word, which was utter nonsense, of course. That word had been on her mind from day one, obviously and how could it not. It was, though, the first time the dreaded word slipped out of her mouth.

"Is it cancer?"

"I'm sorry, but at this early stage, yours is not a diagnostic visit. Due to what you yourself have registered and what I have confirmed, all I can do is refer you to the relevant department. And that process I have put in motion."

"But, from your experience, does it feel like cancer?"

"I'm sorry. One growth feels very much like any other, whether malignant or not. Honestly, I can understand your concern and impatience. However, I am unable to provide you with a clear indication without committing myself and possibly giving you reasons for either false hope or unnecessary worries. You shall be invited for a scan at the earliest opportunity."

During the final sentence, the doctor rose and reached out her hand as a gesture to conclude the consultation and prepare for her next patient.

CHAPTER FOUR

Sleep had come easier that first week after the GP visit. The daily dose of red wine had been halved and sleeping tablets had been made redundant. Each time she had felt the lump, she'd been barely bothered whether it grew or not, convinced that she had made the right move now and that they would fix it if anything should need fixing.

The second week had differed immensely. Although circumstances were exactly the same, seven days after the consultation her worries began, once again, to take the upper hand. The previous dose of wine and pills had been reinstated, but had had little impact on her nights' rest. Rims appeared underneath her eyes and had darkened and deepened at such a slow pace, that she hadn't noticed it herself. Not until a colleague had asked her, whether something was amiss.

Strictly speaking, he was not a colleague, but her senior, Dominique Meesters, the Assistant Branch Manager and one rank higher in the bank's hierarchy, where she was one of the thirty odd cashiers.

She had evaded the question, had payed a visit to the toilet as soon as possible and had taken a long time to examine her face scrutinisingly. In order to avoid suspicion, she'd flushed unnecessarily, once she'd figured out why he had asked the question.

The revelation had shocked her. Never had she expected that already the not knowing would show such an effect so suddenly. What if she'd get the dreaded diagnosis? Then the knowing, doubtlessly, would engrave her face far more strongly, deepen the lines and she would doubtlessly age prematurely. A thirty five year young woman ought not to have any wrinkles. Who wanted her then? That very question had played on her mind often, incessantly often.

Yes, who would want her? Once she was going to be sentenced to scans and tests and treatments, and the devastating rigmarole of chemotherapy and radiotherapy and, finally, surgery. Twice most likely with first mastectomy and to conclude it all, reconstructive surgery. However clever the medical profession might be, scars would remain visible and then only the one breast.

Which man would want her during these months or years of medical procedures? Her life was destined to become dependent on consultants, oncologists, radiologists, GP's, and hospital schedules. These were going to fill her diary. Possible dates, going to a pub and meals out, she could forget about for a long time coming. And by the time the entire ordeal lay in the past, she'd be ancient and had passed her sell-by-date, if she'd survive at all.

Which man would want a woman over thirty five? Worse, which man would want a scarred woman over thirty five? Worse still, which man would want a scarred woman over thirty five with only one breast to fondle and only one nipple to squeeze? After Barry had left, no guy had given her the looks anyway.

Did she want him to know of her predicament? He didn't need to, of course. It might only be a bother to him, because he had well and truly erased her out of his life and had bedded a new girl within a month. She had seen them together just the once. Honestly, what did he see in her with her spiky thin hair, upper teeth like a rabbit and those fat piggy legs. Her inner thighs rubbed against each other with each waddling step. How he ever fitted in between these trunks, she couldn't get her head around, because he wasn't thin either. They looked happy enough, strangled in tight embrace whilst walking.

Had he ever walked this close and intimate with herself? Not that she could remember.

Well over three years they'd been a couple. She had put all her hopes on the relationship lasting, wanted him to make her pregnant and had asked several times, whether he'd move in with her or the other way around or whether they were going to buy or rent somewhere together. Looking back, he had never fully committed. His answers had been consistently vague and evasive. At the same time, never had he said anything to the contrary. His favourite reply had been: "Darling, just don't rush yourself, myself or ourselves, will you please?"

And then, out of the blue, he had sent her that text:

"Sorry darling, but I want to end our relationship. I know it will be hard on you, but I need my freedom."

When she'd received and read it, the sun had been shining, but suddenly it all went dark in front of her eyes. She'd nigh on fainted. The blow had been so strong, that never again had she been able to listen to the Paulo Nutini CD "Sunny side up" with the lyrics:

"He broke her heart on a warm and sunny day
"Oh, he broke her heart on a warm and sunny day
"When she heard what he had to say
"All her sunshine went away
"He broke her heart on a cold and rainy day

Uninvited Guest, Unexpected Gifts

That single text had been all and had remained all. Not a
squeak more had she received. No further explanation he had
given. Not a single reaction there had been to any of her texts,
answering machine messages or e-mails and she'd sent many,
many a day, and often day after day. Whether he had read
them or listened to them or whether he'd deleted the lot, she
would probably never know. For him the episode was finished
with that one text and that after three years of togetherness. He
had always come across as a black or white kind of guy. But
then, if he'd wanted his freedom so badly, why dive straight
into bed with a new girl within a few weeks? Despite that
spiky hair, her rabbit teeth and pigs' thighs she must have
some appeal to lure her Barry into her claws. Sex, most likely.
How else did a woman attract a man and keep him tied to her
side?

Sex involved breasts, both breasts and for them to be perfect
and perfectly healthy. She knew all about it, being raised in a
family, where the daily newspaper traditionally showed a
generous pair of boobs on page three, the eternal and essential
female window display. At the academy most girls had
developed much sooner than she. Also then she'd had sleepless
nights and prayed for them to please, please hurry up and
grow big. And once they had started, there'd been no holding
them back. She remembered, how her mum had cried out in
despair, because of the sheer speed with which they were
growing and her need for bigger size bras yet again. Less than
half a year it had taken her to change from a totally flat to a
firm and generous bust. It had been such a shock to suddenly
have a totally new body, at least that's what it had felt like.

It had also been a shock to people around her. Uncles, whom
she met only once or twice a year, had quickly averted their
eyes downwards in apparent disbelief with pupils flitting from
right to left and back again several times. The traditional pecks
on cheeks had no longer sufficed for them. They'd wanted to
hug her and hold her just a touch longer than customary.

She had been desired. Her window display had made her

desirable. In order to get used to her treasures, as she'd proudly called them, she had stroked her breasts in a nightly ritual, replacing prayer. When the growth subsided, her mirror image showed a beautifully rounded symmetry and when she danced naked in front of the mirror, they danced with her and when she shook her upper body, they shook with her. She'd loved it. She had loved them then and still did.

And now this blow, which had arrived just as unexpected as Barry's text. What had she done to deserve such misfortune? She lived a normal life, as all normal people around her. They didn't receive such a devastating text and they didn't have something hard and suspicious growing in their breasts. Well, of course, some did, but only a few, an odd exception. And she? She faced both, a double whammy.

When thoughts along these lines dumped her back into depression, she did her utmost best not to sink any deeper by telling herself that she had not been diagnosed. No, she had not been diagnosed, yet. She only had something hard growing in her breast. She'd only been to the health centre for a precautionary visit and the GP had not diagnosed her. She also had not been undiagnosed, but surely, if the doctor had had any suspicion of the lump being malignant, she would have rung the alarm bell by now and would have put her file on top of the pile so to speak, but an appointment for a scan still hadn't been forthcoming and she interpreted that as good news.

Yet.

The three letter word "yet" played a crucial role. Each time the mind tried to convince her that she hadn't been diagnosed, that very same mind attempted to glue that tiny word at the back of each sentence. A tiny word, bearing huge significance. These three letters made all the difference between peace of mind and sleepless nights. Only three letters. Never before had she been aware of the importance of one word more or less or of three letters more or less. Such a detail might have intrigued her, had it not been for the level of worry attached to it all.

Attached to those three letters was, in her mind, another three letter word: "Mum". During the last nine years, after her mother had died, she'd rarely allowed her mind access to that word. Like she wanted to push the growth in her breast far, far away into the deep, inaccessible recesses of hidden thoughts, then she had wanted to do the same with mum's illness and suffering. Now even more so, when both seemed to have joined forces to undermine her mood. Although, never in a million years did she suspect her mum of any deliberate act to undermine her happiness.

Mum had always supported her. In everything really. In fact, mum had been the only one who'd been consistently at her side, despite her own deep sorrow and grief, which she had never come to terms with, up to the point, that, when she lay on her deathbed, she'd whispered in her daughter's ear to promise hand on heart to commemorate Robin's birthday, each year.

That had been the exact word her mum had used: commemorate. Not "remember". War victims were being commemorated annually. They, who had paid the ultimate price, whereas Robin had not been in a war zone, but mum had been on a battlefield of a birthing. She would have been bleeding to death if the doctors had not applied some unusual emergency measures. What these had entailed, she wouldn't ever know. Mum had bluntly refused to disclose any hint of the truth and taken mother's and son's secret into the grave with her.

All in all, that had been the horror story of her life, mum's secrets and later that marathon illness with a gruesomely slow decline and an agonising dying process. There'd been three long and dragging on years between mum's first diagnosis and her final breath. It had been three years of helplessness for herself and her dad. Any initial hopes of a positive outcome were being annihilated step by step.

The woman who'd been lying in the marriage bed

throughout, had turned gradually into a stinking semi-corpse, refusing to surrender. Perfume, Eau de Cologne, incense, open windows, any attempts to make their home more liveable had been to no avail. The sickening smell of decay had escaped through the eternally closed door and had penetrated every other room in the house. Mum's deterioration and fear of death had followed husband and daughter deep into their nostrils and had overshadowed every useless effort to make her comfortable. Only morphine had been capable of that, in the end the maximum dose.

During the final months, drinking and eating had been out of the question. However often the bedding had been changed and district nurses had visited to adjust mum's position, bedsores became rife and added their smell to that of urine and decaying breast tissues.

All that had retained its function until the very end, was mum's mind, which had ruled the roost. She'd refused to die in either a hospital or a hospice and wanted, at all cost, to die at home with her husband and her daughter at either side, holding hands. All they'd been capable of doing, had been to respect mum's final wishes and make the best of it.

It had pushed both to alcohol. Never excessively so, but still. Dad had drunk bottle after bottle of Bell's and she herself G & T, strong ones. Each tipple had been accompanied by the promise, that they'd stop as soon as the ordeal would be done and dusted and that promise had been kept.

After the solemn funeral under a leaden sky in thick drizzle, after the gathering had huddled close together around the gaping grave to find shelter from the icy storm, after barely controllable umbrellas had come close to poking out many an eye, after the customary tea, cakes, sandwiches and condoling sentences and handshakes, the widower and his daughter had returned home, had opened as many windows as seemed feasible considering the storm in order to blow mum's smell also heavenwards and had drunk until all bottles had been emptied. The drinking spree had not been a joint decision. It had just happened as an action so self evident, that any discussion or agreement had been superfluous.

The next day's watery sunshine had befitted their bleary eyes and sore heads. Mum had remained central in both their lives, but for a few months only, except when needing to sort out the occasional legal and practical matters.

Was it any wonder, with such a nigh well uninterrupted whirlpool of scarring memories, that her overly active mind was being sucked lower and lower, deeper and deeper into the dark voids of depression? Snowdrops appeared in parks, but her eyes failed to notice their tender beauty and promise at the end of the winter. Each ray of sunshine radiated a touch more warmth than the previous day, but her skin failed to notice the caress. Each evening a blackbird began to serenade her, but her ears failed to notice its joy and gratitude. Her senses shut down or were being shut down by a mind, which preoccupied itself solely with that whirlpool of scarring memories and its consequences.

And when, towards the end of week four, the dreaded letter arrived, she jotted the day and time of the appointment in her diary, as if on automatic pilot without any emotions attached.

She figured that she would need to inform Dominique again. Did he also need to know the reason of her absence? That, in essence simple, question added itself to the downward spiral of self torturing mind games, which had, by that time, undermined any chance of a good night's sleep for close to half a year in a relentless series of anxiety attacks, culminating in ever increasing headaches. Rising, showering, getting dressed, preparing and eating breakfast and commuting were gradually turning into a nightmare of obligations, one piled upon the other.

Work turned into a distraction, dominated by absent-mindedness. Evenings and weekends filled themselves with worries and not much else besides the practicalities of household chores. She invented any excuse under the sun to stay at home at all times, except for work and the necessary grocery shopping.

Life became as she had anticipated: devoid of pub visits, meals out or any other fun events, even before the actual diagnosis and any scheduled hospital appointments. What was life going to be like, once she'd been diagnosed for real and the regime of consultations and treatments had begun? But then again, she had not been diagnosed ..... yet.

Uninvited Guest, Unexpected Gifts

CHAPTER FIVE

"Good morning, Dominique. Are you very busy this morning or can I have a word?"

She had repeated the sentence over and over in her head from the moment the alarm clock switched to Classic FM, throughout the regular morning rituals, all the way from tube station to tube station, until she had entered the building and bumped into the assistant branch manager.

"I'm sure I can spare some minutes. At ten I'll be in a meeting for ….. let's see ….. no longer than half an hour, I reckon. After that? So say, ten forty five in my office?"

As usual his hands spoke alongside his voice. His soft and suave voice sounded as delicate as the chocolates tasted from his compatriots, the Belgian hot chocolate café and chocolaterie just around the corner from where she lived. His relaxed manner never failed to put her at ease or turn her on or both. This time round, only the former, for the turn-on compartment had been incapable of getting activated during these last weeks.

After an hour and a half of prolonged agony, the knock on Dominique's door had a similar effect on her as when she had knocked on that of the GP's consulting room. A queasy tightening made her stomach grumble in protest. For the second time she was forced to own up to her predicament and now, with her diary containing the first hospital appointment, it all became more and more part of an unavoidable reality. Her knees buckled with the prospect, but managed to keep her upright, but only just, it seemed. Her legs dragged her over the doorstep to the nearest chair and immediately with her head leaning forward and sheer willpower overriding the shakiness, the question burst forth without further ado.

"Can I have a day off next Wednesday?"

"Can't see why not, but let's first check the rota."

Their eye contact lingered a touch longer than absolutely necessary and his quizzing gaze felt penetrating.

At least, that's how it came across for the woman, who felt on edge anyway. Her manager's silent quizzing made her squirm, she dropped her eyelids and her throat flushed red. Sweat tickled between both breasts. The thought that that might soon be a thing of the past made a shiver run through her spine. The chill and sweat combined increased her discomfort. She felt smelly, inside as well as outside.

Tension had always flushed her throat red and had made her sweat, especially between her breasts. She'd hated the clamminess. Maybe she ought to learn to treasure it and switch her perception from nuisance to privilege now that she still could.

Dominique's eyes were kind, when he looked up from the screen and said, that there was no problem regarding her request. Had she planned something fun for the day?

"I've got a hospital appointment."

"Nothing serious, I hope?"

"Don't think so. It's just a routine check up. The GP thought

I'd better have a scan, just to make sure."

With each word her voice thinned in insecurity.

"To make sure of what, if you don't mind me asking?"

She was unable to reply.

"What's the matter? Are you OK? You have not been yourself latterly, as if you don't get enough sleep. Is something troubling you? Are you ill? Why do you need a scan?"

The soft Belgian voice spoke very quietly and left her plenty of space to react in between each sentence and question, but no verbal reaction was forthcoming, only a deeper crimsoning of her throat and averted eyes. Two trickling tears accentuated the ensuing silence.

They were the tears of a self-imposed solitude pierced by a caring voice from a caring person. She had felt so lost and alone in her predicament. Not daring to face the truth, she had kept her worries isolated from her acquaintances and in doing thus, she had isolated her innermost self from all and sundry. In doing thus, she had deliberately kept her innermost secret to herself and had dragged it along, in her heart, on her shoulders, in her chest, like an all-encompassing, all-absorbing cross, too heavy to carry for one person alone. The unexpected predicament had occupied her mind day and night and had drained any sense of fun or pleasure or relaxation out of her. It had downgraded her into a probably very, very ill person and had labelled her as a possibly terminally ill youngish woman with an inevitable death sentence hanging over her head.

The sequence of cause and effect had entangled her in a web of stress and tension without her actually realising it. Well, she did realise that sleep came only after alcohol and tablets, but that was all basically. And now that Dominique showed a genuine concern, because he was that the kind of guy, the walls of isolation collapsed around her. She couldn't help herself. Her berating inner voice protested initially:

"What will he think of me? I'll make a mess of the mascara. I can't turn into a sobbing wreck in front of him, at work of all places, at work. I am making a right fool of myself."

37

However, the dam burst.

Despite his caring nature, his soft inviting voice, apparently the assistant manager did not know how to practically comfort a woman. He was young and maybe inexperienced or maybe the more formal work environment held him back.

Whatever his reason might have been, she experienced Dominique's disappointing non-effort as a message to pull herself together. It also showed her the man's inadequacy, where she had previously put him on a pedestal of male competence in matters, both work and women related. In her perception, he dropped deep, from a romantically inclined foreigner to a normal man, unable to give a woman what she needed when she needed it most.

She fished a tissue out of her bag, blew her nose, dabbed her eyes and cheeks and stopped crying as if on command. The decisive action interrupted the shocking rhythm of her shoulders and their brief release of bottled up tension.

She thanked him, stood up, left his office and went to the bathroom to powder her nose, so to speak.

Uninvited Guest, Unexpected Gifts

CHAPTER SIX

She arrived almost an hour too early, just to make sure not to
put the department's schedule into jeopardy. Normally she
placed her handbag next to the chair on the floor. This time
she kept it on her lap, so nobody would notice the disgusting
remnants of her chewed fingernails.

The teenage habit of years had been dropped two full
decades earlier. It hadn't been an easy one to break. In the end,
nail varnish had been the only successful remedy. Painting her
nails fiery red each morning went totally against her own taste
really. It made her stand out too much, she thought and judged
it sluttish and cheap, a bit like the check-out girls at Waitrose.
Still, every time a hand rose for its nail to fall victim to her
teeth, she saw red flash up from the corner of her eyes. The
varnish, sluttish as it might have looked, had made her see red,
literally. Obedient as she was and always had been to the laws
of traffic lights, the colour had had the desired effect. After

only three weeks she'd been able to donate the remainder of the varnish to the thrift shop opposite Waitrose. Without being noticed and with a sigh of relief, she had placed the flagon on a bric-a-brac shelf.

This time round she made a conscious choice not to resort to the same tactics through lack of any other outlet for the tension. She couldn't come up with another solution, other than alcohol, naturally. She drank and chewed. She chewed and drank. Sometimes each in turn and sometimes simultaneously. Whatever the sequence, sleep came and gave solace until Classic FM delivered a new dawn of worries. Of the comatose hours in between, she never had the slightest recollection. Each morning found her in bed, but how she had ended up there, she could never remember. She must have been to the toilet and more than once, most likely, but didn't have the foggiest how she had managed that. She no longer brushed her teeth before going to bed and when waking, the mouth felt and tasted yucky, simply yucky and horridly stale. An alcohol induced dryness made her tongue and roof stick together. Worse than that was her nagging guilty conscience of letting herself down and of letting her teeth down, she, who had always looked after them meticulously and never skipped a dental check-up. She'd begun to check frequently, whether her breath started to smell and at work she resorted to mints, overloaded with sugar, obviously and no good for her teeth either, but at least nobody would notice anything.

Nails and teeth and alcohol was the remedy to not think of her breast and its growth 24/7, but there was a price to pay and a high price really. She didn't like her nails any longer and tried to hide them. She didn't like the idea that her teeth were decaying and that she felt utterly unable to do something about it. She didn't like her breasts any longer, because the one might well have started decaying like her teeth. And the other breast, not ..... yet ..... as far as she was aware, but, who knew what really took place inside her body? Nails, teeth and breasts made it seem that her entire physique was falling apart, way before the onset of the normal ageing process.

Nails, teeth, breasts, premature ageing, all of this had been dumped on her plate. She had chosen none of it, however it had chosen her for some strange reason. Why? Why choose her? What had she done to deserve this? The maelstrom of judgements meant that she no longer liked herself and with not liking herself, she expected nobody to like her. Who would like to spend time with a decaying, depressed woman?

Mum wouldn't have minded a single bit and would have supported her, comforted her and maybe would have accompanied her to the hospital appointment today.

Often the train of thoughts ended with mum and without exception tears welled up and were pushed back. She didn't want to be a burden to her or hold her back or interrupt her peace now that she'd finally found it on the other side. Had mum found peace actually? My God, she hoped so. After all, it had been a long time since dad had closed her eyes. Nine years to be precise and mum deserved peace and needed it.

And now, she herself faced a similar fate without a husband or a daughter to look after her or be at her bedside during those final stages.

Unobtrusively, she hoped at least, her eyes wandered through the waiting room and noticed that nobody else had come alone. Her heart began to ache in grief and the realisation made her feel nauseous and she wanted to burp. She suppressed the urge for fear of throwing up and swallowed heavily.

Two older women wore wigs. One man's skull was covered in baby down. These three were patients, obviously, who'd been through the mill and had had chemo or radio therapy or both. One of those women and the man looked incredibly frail, pasty, grey and lifeless. For their accompanying children, at least that's who she assumed they were, they pretended to be upbeat with a sardonic kind of grin suitable for some Halloween film, in the hope it came across as a genuine smile.

Then there was this female trio, apparently mother and two

daughters. She couldn't fathom who was patient and who had come in support. They giggled incessantly and tried not to, or at least tried not to disturb the laden, whispered silence of a group of people, who had been thrown together for an unwanted purpose. The three could not help themselves and giggled behind hands and elbows and when one ended up hiccuping, there was no holding them back.

The laughter was infectious in as far that it actually managed to make a few people smile, some genuinely and some sardonically. One couple looked ever so harsh with quickly flitting glances in the direction of the trio.

A woman entered, supported by a man, probably her husband, because both wore similar rings. She was skin over protruding bones with an ashen skin colour. He did his best to keep a cloth in front of her face. When she stumbled, the soaked cloth moved and fresh blood showed in and around her mouth.

No chair was vacant and the man with downy hair stood up for her, whilst he himself needed to lean heavily against the wall.

The husband nodded in gratitude.

No word was exchanged and the scene accentuated the tense silence.

She could have given the woman her seat. It hadn't crossed her mind. The man, however weak, had shown more composure. Should she now return the gesture and sacrifice her seat for his comfort? The atmosphere seemed too stifling to move and even non-verbal communication would disturb the heavy quietude, which required to be maintained, as if decreed by some unwritten law. Besides that, she would need to stand up, thereby stand out and be noticed.

In response, she withdrew back into her shell, averted her eyes and stopped all observations. Every time somebody stood up and left or somebody new arrived, curiosity cried out to be satisfied. It took real effort to remain shielded, for, by now, she wanted to include all these strangers into her world, although, nobody was going to introduce her to them or vice versa. If she wished to become acquainted with any of them, she'd have to take the initiative to start a conversation. That felt too huge a risk to take.

She had let Dominique in on her secret. He was a decent kind of guy from the continent without the usual English reservedness and she'd made herself vulnerable in front of him. OK, with him being her senior, she had needed to approach him to get time off, but there'd really been no need to unburden herself. Not that she had taken advantage of the situation, but still, she'd cried buckets in front of him and had made a real fool of herself. And, had he shown any sympathy? Not a single shred. Had he come across and put a hand on her shoulder? Forget it. Not a single word he had uttered. Also not afterwards. He had never addressed the issue again and it felt like he was avoiding her. So much for reaching out.

In the waiting room she found herself surrounded by people in the same boat. They all had something huge in common and part of her wished she had the courage to reach out. She didn't want to be left alone with her worries all any longer. At the same time, she didn't dare to stand out and make a fool of herself, like she'd done with Dominique. Besides that, all the other patients had company, so why should they bother with her? Each carried their own burden and had no need for hers on top of it all.

She waited.

Tjitze de Jong

CHAPTER SEVEN

The receptionist recognised her, or, at least, she remembered which GP she came to see and told her to take a seat.

"It wont be a minute."

As a distraction, her thoughts meandered over that receptionist's frequently abused phrase, implying that the expected waiting time was going to be less than that minute. In that respect, the phrase proved to be always wrong. One minute equaled sixty seconds and each time the phrase was uttered as a softening of the fact that waiting was required and time was lost, it turned out to be a straightforward lie, namely, that implication and expectation were not being met, never. Never did the promised event occur within the sixty seconds time lapse. Never ever. Therein lay the lie.

Still, the statement was true. Always. The time lapse was never exactly sixty seconds, but always longer. Always and forever.

Uninvited Guest, Unexpected Gifts

From the seat she'd chosen, she had an uninterrupted view of the now familiar screen with scrolling letters comprised of red dots. She waited and stared.

Staring ahead in apathy, she was oblivious to the fact, that, after several times sixty seconds, Gwyneth entered. She looked around, spotted her friend, went and stood next to her without being noticed and tried to get her attention. When words fell on deaf ears, she gently placed a hand on her friend's shoulder.

The effect of the physical touch was, literally, startling.

"So sorry ... did I miss my turn again?"

Big, round eyes looked up in an astonished fear, as if she expected to be scolded.

"Oh, it's you. Hi, Gwyneth. Nice to see you. How are you doing?"

One soprano took a seat next to the other.

They were the two sopranos in the choir of twelve of which she was secretary and treasurer. She had joined over three years ago when there'd been only five members. They had practised, experimented and sang purely for pleasure. Within half a year she had been urged to become treasurer, because the informal structure no longer sufficed, when, out of the blue, four others had asked to be included, Gwyneth one of them. The majority had voted for formalising the organisation a bit in order to grow, in numbers as well as in prestige, from a small group joining voices fortnightly for the sheer fun of it to weekly practise in preparation for a series of performances in public.

The new set up, as well as her newly acquired function, had taken her totally by surprise. She had agreed, also because computer literacy seemed second nature.

For that reason alone, at work, she could have been promoted to assistant manager had it not been for the other contestant, Dominique, to be a man, albeit from a Glaswegian branch and already part of the existing team.

He had never known that he'd pipped her at the post and she

45

wouldn't enlighten him, nor hold it against him. It wasn't his fault, after all, that he had been born a boy and she a girl, unfair as it was.

With him, management did not run the risk of work commitments being interrupted due to pregnancy. With her, there wouldn't have been any risk either, she'd thought then already, cynically. Who would want her anyway, virtually an old spinster? That self image was changing radically, for the worse.

Management was not to know that, naturally, not then, not now and they would never be in the know.

When the choir treasurer's husband had received a pretty radical and seemingly unexpected promotion, he and his family had moved abroad.

And when almost all choir members had been of the opinion, that both positions would be best held under the same umbrella and had thought her the most suitable candidate, she'd gone along with it without questioning. The group had been small, engagements a rarity and the work involved minimal, initially. She'd manage both functions easily, initially.

The three male members, though, had instigated a change of repertoire, away from happy singsonging along with middle of the road material from ABBA, Beatles, Robbie Williams, Titanic and the like. The trio, christened by the female contingent as the three tenors, had been blown away by a six people small amateur choir, performing the choral Finale of Beethoven's Ninth Symphony at the Edinburgh Festival. Not even bothering to inform the women, they'd taken the initiative to contact a retired conductor and one evening had surprised all women by arriving as a group, with him in tow.

There'd been no singing whatsoever that night. It had turned into a late, late night filled with discussions, more discussions and only that, discussions. For her it had been by far the worst night in the choir's history. And yes, she could see the point that their repertoire was limited and that their capacities were not nearly stretched one tenth of an inch, let alone to the limit.

It had also been the first time, she'd been singled out as the member with the most far reaching voice amongst them. How they had come to that idea, she'd never know, for she hadn't dared to ask. Although, there'd been a unanimous agreement.

She'd always loved to sing. When she was little, there'd been no stopping her if she had had it her own way. Lyrics were absorbed effortlessly by listening to a song only the once and it made no difference, whether it was pop, rock, jazz, classic, nor did the language matter. Words just got stuck in her brain somehow. What was it with her and words?

So, she'd sung before and after breakfast, before and after lunch, before and after dinner, in the bath, in the shower and in the garden, where she sang with and for the little birds with the bright and cheery innocence of children's enjoyment with a spring in her step and a twinkle of pure unadulterated happiness in her eyes and with the high, shrill voice of her age, albeit steadfast in lyrics and rhythm,

Talented, had said uncles and aunties, in front of whom she'd performed without being asked or prompted, but because she'd wanted to share her joy with them too.

She must have been about five when it had all changed. She'd sung a duet with a high pitched chaffinch. The bird knew an unimaginable repertoire and had had a combination of variations on a theme available from its tiny throat, she'd never ever in her wildest dreams be capable of. She'd done her best, though, positioning herself underneath the tree where the bird had been perched. The finch had flown a branch lower. There, in the garden, under the flowering white lilac, surrounded by its scent, in mutual adoration with the delicately coloured chaffinch, she had given it her all, as had the birdie. The finch had flown yet another branch lower. The two had been locked in a contest of who'd be able to give both the other and the self the most pleasure. The finch had flown onto the lowest branch, directly above her head, a head lopsided in concentration. The celebratory auras of both girl and bird had encompassed the entire garden as well as the neighbouring ones.

One neighbour had ventured outside and listened, not knowing what to make of a combination of sounds he had not come across before. The thick two meter high conifer hedge had blocked his view and he'd been left wondering. The man had hastened back inside a few minutes later.

The unlikely duo had ended up in an enchanted world, liberated by a spontaneous sharing of heart and soul. It had made no difference, that the one had been human and the other animal. Exhilaration had crossed all boundaries. If she'd been able to ascend, she would have seated herself in touching distance. Instead, she'd stretched her arm and had held out her hand, palm up, inviting the finch to descend.

Its tiny wings had fluttered in sitting. Would it have dared to cross a boundary which no other chaffinch had dared cross before? And when bravery had won, the tiny wings had lifted the small body off the branch and had lifted the girl's heart in adoration.

She had noticed somehow the hesitation, the excitement and the sheer courage of her feathered friend and had sung with an inviting sweetness. Sung? Could those deep throated sounds of sweetness have been called singing? In turn soft and loud the voice had sounded. Ever so gently the one hand waved rhythmically where there'd been no rhythm. Each wave had played the harp strings of her heart on vocal cords. It had been as if fingers had drawn the finch ever closer, ever further beyond the conditioned border of an inbred fear of humans. She'd no longer sung. It had been a cooing, a tempting, a shrieking, all in all an uncensored melee of vocal expressionism as a string of variations on a non-existent theme.

And when the minuscule wings had made the final move towards the outstretched arm and the girl's heart had lifted and the feathered body had fluttered in the direction of that inviting human hand, the duet had finished into a harsh crescendo of unexpectedness during which a third voice had blown it all to pieces, had shattered a girl's dream and had confirmed a chaffinch's fear of people.

"What are you doing?"

The "are" had been accentuated.

After hearing the attack, the neighbour had closed the door so as not to intrude.

She had never before encountered a bird from such close quarters and had never sang this intimately with a bird before. She had never met a friend before with whom she'd been able to sing this freely. She'd never experienced such a thrill before in all her five years.

She had also never before heard such a sharpness in her mother's voice. Like a butcher's knife, after the whetstone's sparks had been flying in celebration, the killing edge had sliced through thin air, separating entwined auras and cutting cords in a scarring disruption of the magic both had ensued, created and savoured.

A tirade of "consideration for neighbours", "you can't call that singing", "what a noise you're making" and such like, had followed.

She'd hurt, deeply, in her wide open, singing and sharing heart. From then on she had stopped calling her mother "Mother" and had referred to her as "Mum" because "Mum" had felt more distant to the little girl, who had from earliest memory associated the title "Mother" with the intimate bond they had shared for five whole years. It had been the word mum had taught her and therefore chosen for daughter to address herself, honouring the person who had given birth to her, suckled her and was raising her. Of course, the little girl's brain hadn't figured out this train of thoughts rationally. Her instinct had made the shift happen somehow and it had stuck.

Whether her mother had ever consciously noticed the change of words or not, she definitely had never touched the subject.

In the waiting room the newcomer was first to ask: "What are you here for?"

"Oh, well ….. eh ….. they're going to give me some scan results. What about you?"

"Same here. Are going back to work after this?"

"No, I took the whole day off."

"Me too."

Her surname flashed in red.

"There we go. That's me."

"Shall we wait for each other afterwards and maybe go for a coffee somewhere?"

"Yeah, let's. See you in a bit then."

She went to the indicated consultation room.

Uninvited Guest, Unexpected Gifts

CHAPTER EIGHT

Together with bringing the cappuccino for Gwyneth and the
hot chocolate for herself, it was as if the waiter also fired the
starting pistol for serious interaction to commence. Up to then
discussions had evolved around the weather, last and this
week's rehearsals and the rather daunting concert in a
fortnight's time. All three topics covered safe ground and were
agreed upon before a word was spoken. No sooner did the
waiter place the items on the table, including a bill which
hadn't been asked for, then one soprano asked about the other's
scan results.

The other stirred foam counter clockwise and stared into its
epicentre. What had been highly embarrassing in front of
Dominique, happened a second time. At snail's pace a pair of
tears drew a downward track on each cheek. Then she looked
up and said: "I'm not ready to talk about it yet. Not yet. What
about you? You first."

Gwyneth's mouth opened to utter some automated response. She thought better of it, sipped cappuccino and placed the cup back on its saucer, deep in thought about how little they knew of each other, other than some musical preferences. Once before, on her own initiative, they'd gone for a drink after rehearsals. That was all in the almost three years they'd been acquainted. Then, their conversation had circled around men, with mutually non-committal questions, answers and remarks. Now, something more sinister lay around the corner judging by the other woman's response. She decided for the diplomatic approach and go easy on her friend and not display too much of her own celebratory mood after receiving the all-clear.

"For the last few weeks I felt a pain in my groin, somewhere in the region of the right ovary or just below. Initially I thought I'd overstretched a muscle with aerobics or something like that. It didn't go away though and it felt as if it was growing."

"Were you scared?"

"A bit."

"Did all kind of thoughts about worst case scenarios follow you around? In your mind? All the time?"

"Pretty much, yes. One day after a really bad night's sleep I went to see my GP. She prodded a bit and sent me for a scan. That was last week."

"And the result?"

"It is an innocent cyst apparently. She gave me the choice to have it surgically removed if it keeps growing and gives more discomfort. Otherwise, it may shrink on its own accord in due course and fade away altogether."

"Lucky you."

"Guess so. It is a great relief to know there's no malignancy. I never thought it would be the case, but one never knows these days. There's so much of it about. The GP would like me to have another check-up in about half a year's time, just to make sure. Unless, of course, I decide to go for the operation."

"Will you?"

Uninvited Guest, Unexpected Gifts

"Go for the operation? Don't think so. I don't want to drag my body through such an ordeal if it's not necessary."

"I'd do the same, if I were you."

"What about you? You also received scan results?" and when the woman opposite nodded: "Gosh, is it epidemic or something? Was your news worse than mine?"

"Unfortunately, yes. Sorry, I didn't mean to imply that I'd wish this upon you, but ….."

"I understand, silly. Have you been diagnosed with ….?

"With cancer? Yes. YES! I have been diagnosed with cancer. I have been diagnosed with cancer. I have been diagnosed with cancer."

Each time the voice became softer. Each time words and syllables were pronounced slower.

"Yes, Gwyneth, I have been diagnosed with cancer. I'd better try and get used to the idea that I've got cancer."

"Gosh, you. I'm so so sorry to hear this. Don't know what to say really. Here's me getting in the mood to celebrate the all-clear and at the very same time, you ….."

"At the very same time, indeed. Ironic or what, our meeting and the timing of it all. Don't get me wrong, I'm glad for you, mightily glad for you, but my life has been blown apart."

"Can they still do something for you?"

"Oh yes, loads. That's part of the problem. They want me to make up my mind as soon as possible. Once I give them the go ahead, life will be dominated by doctors, oncologists, radiologists, surgeons. The GP explained it all. What they can do. What my options are. But, to be honest, most of it went over my head. She rattled through an overwhelming avalanche of information all at once, when all I felt was shock. Pure shock. Even though, I had expected it to be the case."

Her hands rummaged through her handbag and reappeared with some papers, whilst she spoke.

"Are these the brochures they gave you? Great. Then you can quietly take your time, relax and read them at your leisure. And talk it over with some friends. They'll help you."

She let out a deep sigh, not knowing who those 'they' might be and where she'd find anybody who would be willing to help her pick up the pieces. It was easy talking for Gwyneth, who had received the all-clear and who ought to be celebrating instead of being bothered by her and her misery. Maybe all was not lost and she'd somehow end up at the other end of the tunnel, the brighter side of the tunnel. Somehow she'd have to get through it.

"I guess you're right. At the moment it all feels a very daunting prospect."

"I can well imagine."

Gwyneth looked at her mobile. It was clear, that the surprise element in her expression was feigned, when she uttered a sopranoesque squeak about needing to meet someone somewhere in no time at all. Brusquely she stood up, put a feather light hand on the other woman's shoulder, pecked a hasty gesture on one cheek and told her not to worry. It would all be OK. They would meet again in two days for choir practise and might go for a drink afterwards, if she'd like that. The whirlwind dumped a few pound coins on the table and hurried towards freedom. Hordes on the pavement swallowed her.

To become relegated from together to alone had taken less than half a minute. She was left speechless. If this was what friendship was like when in dire straits, it wasn't worth taking the risk of getting involved with anybody and unburdening herself into a humiliating vulnerability. First Dominique at work. Now Gwyneth from choir. Both seemed decent enough people, especially he, but both ended up disappointing her and hurting her into a deep disappointment. None of the two had even asked what kind of cancer she had or how serious it was. Disclosing her predicament created loneliness, a terrible loneliness. She felt terribly lonely after having revealed the secret, that became as clear as a bell.

"Sod it", had been mum's favourite expression. She had used it often during her illness, when prognoses had turned into a death sentence. It had been the ultimate swearword for a woman who never swore.

"Sod it sod it sod it sod it sod it sod it sod it sodsodsodsod it."

Tjitze de Jong

CHAPTER NINE

The door knocker dropped with quite an explosive bang. She
never knew how hard or soft to handle the solid brass, hand
shaped thing.

The eternal joke was, that her stepmum had paid for solar
panels to be installed on the roof when she'd moved in, to help
reduce his bills, whilst he had replaced the electric bell with a
knocker in order to safe even more electricity.

Charlie answered the door and invited her in. Always
Charlie. Never did dad himself welcome his only daughter.
Why not, she often wondered, especially when they knew it to
be her arrival and no one else's, because she never failed to
ring beforehand. She would love to know whose decision it
had been or if it was always her who answered to door no
matter who arrived. Or was it one of her not so subtle ways of
worming herself in between boyfriend and stepdaughter,
something she'd had a knack of right from the word "go",

three months after mum's death. Three months only. From the very beginning they had shown demonstratively how deeply they'd fallen in love, which was a big joke really, a sour joke steeped in disloyalty as far as daughter was concerned.

Whatever mum might or might not have deserved, definitely not to be deleted out of her husband's life within three months of him closing her eyes. That final physical act had seemed such an intimate deed to witness, a symbol of marriage until death parted husband and wife forever, after sharing all ups and downs and weathering life's storms together. Dad's gesture had totally taken daughter by surprise and the tender gesture stood engraved in her memory, her vivid memory of mum's final breath. She treasured the moment ever since, as a confirmation that all had been harmonious between her parents on the level of love, whatever disagreements life had thrown at them over the years and here'd been many. Him closing her eyes as his last service to his loyal wife had made all previous fights fade into insignificance for the grieving and witnessing daughter.

The traditional embrace and peck on both cheeks was just that, tradition, lacking any closeness. Charlie strode ahead, opened the living room door and announced daughter's arrival. That's how she'd always addressed her: "your daughter" with a strange kind of emphasis on the word "daughter". An emphasis, which had caused an ongoing unpleasant feeling deep down in the guts of that same daughter each time she heard it repeated without being able to put an exact finger on why.

It was a fact that after Charlie had entered dad's life and home, daughter had never been able to spend more than a couple of minutes alone with him. He didn't seem to either notice or mind.

As soon as the staple diet of Nescafe and McVities had arrived, she took her chance before step mum had the opportunity to start one of her long winded, boring stories about nothing in particular.

She angled her body towards her dad, away from Charlie, when she said, she'd been to see the doctor.

"Nothing serious, I hope?" butted Charlie in.

"Well, actually, yes, it is serious. Otherwise I wouldn't have disturbed your peace."

She detected the cynical undertone in her own words and hated herself for it. Her eyes didn't avert nor did her body turn and she spoke only to her father, if at all possible, when she announced the diagnosis, including the word "breast" to try and create a deja vu effect in him.

Daughter's emphasis wasn't lost on father. His eyes grew big as saucers, before they closed during an erratic intake of breath. Or was it a sob? His facial features contorted into a variety of grimaces, from shock, to fear, to grief, to trying to control, to more fear and more grief.

It made Charlie unable to interfere and she observed her partner as if worried for his well being.

It also made his daughter into a fascinated spectator. Each contortion of her father's face tore her heart apart. She had no idea how much he still suffered underneath the façade, upheld by both him and his girlfriend. A naked agony of the soul suddenly became obvious, whereas she'd been made to believe that Charlie's appearance had smoothed over all cracks of the heart. It hurt to see her father in agony. Simultaneously, his grief did her the world of good, realising that mum hadn't been brushed aside after all and realising also that her own illness pained her father's heart. It proved his love for her, his daughter. Her father loved his daughter and she was that very same daughter. No other conclusion could be drawn. She wanted to drop on her knees in front of him, cry with him and hold him close to make it all better for both.

Charlie's presence and hawk eyed observation prevented her from acting upon her impulse.

Once he had composed himself, he apologised for behaving like a child.

Neither of the two women responded, fully aware of each

other's scrutinising competitiveness and unspoken criticism. Both watched the man, each with their own interpretation. Neither focused on him after he'd pulled himself together. In stead they observed each other in icy suspicion, prepared to pounce, were the competitor to claim her own rightful place at the man's side.

"I will not lose you as well, will I?"

Moist eyes and a distressed voice forced her to come up with a reply filled with confidence, where there was none. She faked it, knew it and hoped he wouldn't notice.

"No daddy, you wont."

There they sat. Father and daughter. Three meters apart. Attached in mutual grief of the dying process of the woman who had been his wife and her mum and at the same time forcefully detached by the woman who was his girlfriend and her stepmum.

The chasm the latter created in the room was of gigantic proportions. Did she recognise it and if she did, did it seal her victory over the woman fifteen years her junior? She watched with her eyes slightly squeezed and a vertical frown engraved above her nose. It accentuated the pointy nose and seemed to sharpen it and grow into the giant beak of a vulture, perched in still, vast surrounds, silhouetted against the sky as a symbol of tranquillity and of a threatening extermination. Only the close observer would notice that stepmum's pupils darted from side to side, forever on the alert.

The room's atmosphere was heavy to say the least.

If he was perfectly frank with himself, he'd want to spend time alone with his daughter and ask Charlie to leave them be for an hour or so, but the thought struck him as extremely disloyal towards his girlfriend. Charlie staying in the room, struck him as extremely disloyal towards his wife and daughter. Never before had he found himself caught in a web of women. He was well aware, that the two of them were not the best of friends, but not enemies either and their relationship had worked out fine really, come to think of it.

There'd been no objections forthcoming when he and Charlie
became an item.

"When did you find out?"

"Just now. I felt a lump in my breast and when it didn't go
away. I thought, I better have it checked. So I went to the
doctor and she sent me for a scan. This morning they gave me
the message. It's malignant. I've got cancer."

"Gosh, that comes as a shock. First ….."

He swallowed deeply.

"…..and now you. What can they do for you?"

"At this stage a lot still, apparently. The doctor explained it
all, but I was in such a shock, that I didn't manage to take it all
in. If I remember rightly, they want to take the lump out and
check if also the lymph nodes have been affected. Or, if I want
to, I can give them permission to remove all lymph nodes,
whether they are cancerous or not. According to her, it can
reduce the risk of cancer spreading, but they can't guarantee
that."

"Can they guarantee anything?"

"No, not really, as far as I am aware."

"Also not that you will live?"

"Don't be so stupid, George. She's not going to die. Look at
her. Look how young and healthy she looks. The two of you
talk as if it's about time to ring the funeral directors. Don't be
so morbid."

"Well, the fact is, that most people with cancer die."

"We must all die at some point."

"But not necessarily before our time."

"How do you know when it is your time? You don't get an
invitation sent from Peter at the pearly gates to come and see
him at such and such a day at such and such an hour, do you?"

"No, but to die before you're thirty isn't right, is it? How old
are you now?"

"Thirty six come July."

"Gosh, are you that old already? Where does time go? Even
at thirty five somebody is far too young to die."

"But, she is not dying and she is not going to die for a long time yet. They invent new medicine all the time. I bet you a thousand pounds, that in ten years time hardly anybody will die of cancer. What did they say in the news last week? A new combination of two already existing drugs showed such promising results, that it had taken the entire research team by surprise. And so the medical expertise will keep moving forward in the foreseeable future."

"They cannot guarantee anything, the doctor said."

"And does your doctor have all the latest information? Of course not. How can he?"

"She."

"Okay, don't get your knickers in a twist. How can she? A GP deals with all manner of medical complaints. They can't possibly have all the latest reports of all ailments at their fingertips. Leave that to the specialists. Your oncologist knows that. Have you got one yet?

"No."

"Well, ask around and find out who's got the best reputation in the area. That's what I would do."

"Who did mum have, dad?"

"Well, you surely don't want that one again. With such a record in the family? You must be joking."

"True enough, Charlie. I don't think I can remember his name anyway. He was quite an abrupt man, to say the least."

"What can I do, dad?"

"Just do what they recommend. They know best and will have your best interest at heart."

"But with mum ….."

"Yes, I know ….."

Whilst he sighed deeply and swallowed, his partner took over once more.

"Well, that episode is nine years ago. Nine years. A lot of water has gone under the bridge since then and a lot of new inventions have been made to prolong the life of people with cancer."

"I don't want my life to be prolonged. I want to rid myself of cancer."

"If you would have let me finish, I was going to add exactly that, that they also have found many cures. Have you got any idea, how many people wander about happily ever after, even with having had cancer? The medical profession does its best, believe you me. Especially with somebody as young and healthy as you are. And you caught it early, didn't you?"

"Guess so."

She didn't dare to admit how many months she had waited, procrastinated, before she'd made the first appointment. That game's setback card had chased her mind all day. Never had she anticipated a mere game to be so accurate and impacting.

"Well then, what's there to worry? Nothing, I'd say. Just let them deal with it. It's their job. Isn't that ultimately why we receive such hefty tax bills? And we pay our fair share, don't we, George?"

"More than, I'd say. I think Charlie is spot on, you know. Try not to worry unduly. What is past is past and it's no good dwelling on it or let your own situation be affected by what happened nine years ago."

Every time they entered a discussion of any significance, which was a rare occurrence, her father ended up in an undisputable agreement with his girlfriend, irrespective of subject or opinions. Every time it filled his daughter with despair. The father, she had once had and loved with all her dedicated daughter heart, that father who had sometimes been embarrassingly opinionated, that father she had looked up to as a little girl, that father who had acted like a rock during mum's illness, that father had died less than nine years ago. For a few months after the cremation she could still rely on him to deal with all practicalities and necessities regarding the estate, the inheritance and whatever else needed sorting. Father and daughter had discussed matters openly and tying up the loose ends had had an air of satisfaction to it, honouring the woman who had occupied such an all-important role in both of their lives. It had softened the pain and hence supported the grieving process. The two had acted as pillars of mutual support in a fashion, that any support from friends and more distant relatives had seemed superfluous.

Together they had lain flowers on the graveyard each Sunday. Together they'd taken the deceased into their prayers on a daily basis. Together they had remembered and reminisced, cried and laughed. Together they'd made pretty useless attempts in cooking mum's favourite meals, feeling supported in mutual failure and had even dared a giggle at each other's expense.

All of that very real sharing of pain. All of that gorgeous grief. All of that positive acknowledgement of her who had passed away and of them who had remained. All of that intimacy caused by death. All of the beauty, which still permeated every word, sentence and phrase uttered on her behalf. All of that and much more besides had created the beauty of love nourished by the courage to express it.

Father and daughter had made shopping lists and gone to the supermarket together. They had decided a daily menu together and prepared meals together. They had held hands together during and after meals. They had sat next to each other on the sofa watching a film or TV. They had gone to bed simultaneously and had embraced the other before entering their own bedroom and had embraced again between bedroom door and bathroom door the next morning.

Neighbours, friends and family members had whispered in harsh judgement, for their behaviour had been deemed abnormal.

Father and daughter had not heard any of these judgements and if they had heard, would they have taken notice?

Those same neighbours, friends and family members had whispered in pleasant surprise three months later when Charlie had arrived on the scene. Although, three months under the most dramatic of circumstances had been deemed not long before a widow started bedding a next woman. However, the new situation had eradicated the previous misconstrued one and there'd been something to say for that, most definitely.

Charlie had taken mum's place, clearly glad with, also, her estate. In that, daughter, neighbours, friends and family had been in agreement. Although none had been in the knowledge of the other's opinion, except, naturally, for the ones who had kept the whispering going. That category had always been in the know and always would be, apparently.

The intimate father-daughter-bond had been, to put it mildly, placed on the back burner, to remain there for as long as Charlie kept devoting her young body, compared to mum's anyhow, to that of a man, fifteen years her senior, who couldn't belief his luck and had made sure he'd dedicated his time, energy and money in the right direction for the newly discovered love to flourish.

In a nutshell: daughter had been dropped.

The new woman didn't exactly rub it in, but she had made sure that junior was going to get used to her relegated position in no time at all. She now held his hands during and after mealtimes, also or especially in daughter's presence. More than just his hands, to be precise.

She had never witnessed any physical intimacy between her parents. A drop in the pecking order combined with the shock of their open display, had made her loose her appetite in more ways than one. Pretty soon she'd explored estate agents' websites and had found her flat, had moved out, had moved into her new abode and had led a life filled with grief, for her mum's physical death as well as for her father's emotional and mental death. She'd felt orphaned, betrayed. She'd lived alone and pretty lonesome. Her circle of friends had been ignored during mum's long lasting illness and those following months. It had seemed too much of an effort to rekindle neglected friendships by taking the initiative herself, so she'd left friendships for what they had turned into, non-existent.

Out of the endless spell of silence arose daughter's insecure voice.

"When I get my appointment for the operation, will you come with me, dad, to the hospital?"

"Why don't you allow me to support you. Your dad will be at work, no doubt. And isn't it more appropriate to be accompanied by a woman, especially when your cancer concerns such an intimate, female body part?"

"I appreciate your kind offer, but I'd love my father to join me, if you don't mind." was the icy reply.

When Charlie averted her eyes and faced her partner, she mumbled something, which distinctly sounded like: "Suit yourself."

"Thank you for asking me and yes, I shall oblige. Although, I'd much rather it be a happier occasion, like giving you away at the altar to the man of your dreams. However, beggars can't be choosers. You know it's often not easy for me to skip work, but I shall see what I can do. Let me know as soon as possible when the appointment is and I'll try and attempt to clear my diary."

"Thank you, dad. It means a lot to me. Really it does."

Tjitze de Jong

CHAPTER TEN

Sunbeams filter through the greenery and paint a pattern of waving shade and light in the grass in front of my feet. I face the sunlight with closed eyes to even feel the pleasant warmth on the delicate skin of my eyelids. Birds flutter from branch to branch alongside me.

When they are a few trees ahead of me on either side of the clover and bee strewn track, they wait and sing, urging me to follow.

It's unnecessary to be urged forward, because each step is a feast, a celebration of the senses, but I love their company, their cheer.

To the left and the right, woods stretch out indefinitely.

I don't recognise the trees' species. All that matters is their exquisiteness and how the canopy lets the light through, creating a filtered magic. The contrast of shadowed patches where a sunbeam reaches a tree trunk and brings it to light amidst a tapestry of tender wood anemones or a clump of waving grasses surrounding a rock covered in moss, together exhibiting every shade of green imaginable. All light drenched colours become more pronounced by surrounding darkness.

I walk through a world Rembrandt could have painted. It ignites the passion of Van Gogh. The master of light joined by the master of the senses in one and the same landscape.

A sunbeam catches a roe deer. The golden brown fur shines, sparkles and adds a feast of different colours to the already overflowing pallet. It will have been running. Its flanks are heaving in a rhythm of fast and deep breathing. Exhaling and inhaling the air has an effect similar to that of the breeze, it continuously changes the patterns of light and dark in the deer's fur in an ever alive mosaic.

I stand still, mesmerised by the sheer gorgeousness of it all. The pure spontaneity of fluctuations in senses being blissfully tickled, surprises me second after second.

And I become my own surprise.

Unbeknown to myself I'd started to sing in a voice lifted to the angelic, lifting me heavenwards amidst earthly splendour. I sing to the deer. I sing to the deer in deep, deep gratitude of soul and heart. I sing to the deer until its tripod antlers change from rusty brown to white, starting at the very tips and slowly slipping as low as the skull.

I observe, utterly amazed, stop singing and begin to think, analyse and conclude the scene's utter impossibility, until, for not wanting to waste the incredibly generous spread of gifts, I override the interrupting mind by singing the line "How can I keep from singing" and continue my previous improvisations.

Then, my jaw drops and my breath halts. However weird it may sound, it doesn't prevent my unnaturally high pitched soprano voice from serenading the deer in variations on the theme of "Amazing Grace." The jaw dropping, breathtaking transformation in front of my eyes can be described as follows:

After the antlers had whitened in their entirety, the process proceeded all over the gracefully lifted head, including the brown tipped nostrils. It was not the white of a painting or a cloud or a dinner plate. Even the description white sparkling snow in frosty February sunshine didn't fully do it justice. The shininess and sparkliness approached transparency. I expected nothing less than to be able to see branches waving behind the deer, straight through its physical appearance, once its neck and body had changed from brown to white. The legs transformed last. And once the deer had swapped its shiny summer coat for one similar to that of a wintry snow hare, shape shifting commenced. Legs lengthened and grew more voluminous, as did the body. A long, wavy tail sprouted out of its behind. The neck thickened into that of a horse. The most startling of all, was the disappearance of the antlers. One second they stood where they belonged and the next, they had vanished. Then, in between and just below the eyes arose the single horn.

In front of me stands a unicorn.

All of nature is awestruck. The wind has dropped. Birds have been silenced. Each tree has changed into a white stemmed birch or something similar. The atmosphere has turned eerily into the total silence of magic. Expectancy hangs thick.

It doesn't move.

I do. I have no choice. Movement somehow turns into immobile locomotion, in between striding and gliding with physically impossible, elongated steps and without my feet touching the forest floor. Although, tips of heather tickle the soles of my feet. Awe fills every bit of me and becomes ever stronger, the closer I get to the creature.

She..... I have no idea whether it's female, though. I have no idea whether unicorns have males or females or whether they even need to in order to procreate. If they materialise in the way I've observed, there ought to be no ground for the male/female division. Imagine that for humankind. Wouldn't that change society?

Uninvited Guest, Unexpected Gifts

She, because everything about her feels feminine in its soft warmth, in its openness and receptivity, also in its stance of strength and empowerment, nods. Not in any approving or disapproving manner, but simply in acknowledgement of me approaching. A strange light shines out of both eyes and holds me in streamers swirling around me and coaxes me in the most positive sense of the word.

Within a meter's distance strides come to a halt. I kneel on one knee. The heather around my legs is not scraggy, but downy soft. I bow my head, unable to stand the intense light streamers from her eyes.

Her left front hoof, it has the softness of a kitten's paw, lifts and raises my head ever so gently. She softens the light's intensity from her eyes a fraction, so I can maintain eye contact again.

Her left front hoof makes me rise. Then she steps back half a meter, bows until her horn reaches out horizontally in my direction and draws a circle around my left breast with its horn. Thrice.

It feels as if the breast detaches itself from the rest of my body and a strange sensation spreads through my chest, as if a hoover is attached to the horn. It tickles, bearably so and I begin to feel uplifted, as if all burdens, shouldered for years, drop off in an instant and seem to evaporate. A lightness takes its place. The effect is especially palpable in my shoulder girdle. Involuntarily I in- and exhale deeply a few times, until it feels as if the breast attaches itself again and I feel complete, more complete than ever.

The unicorn fades away. She doesn't transform back into the roe deer. She simply dissolves.

Also, the birches change back into the previous variety of trees with leaves and branches rustling in the gentle breeze, which picks up once more. Birds start to sing again. Smells are a pure feast to my nostrils.

I start to walk and sing, then dance through the woods, filled with an unfathomable gratitude.

Tjitze de Jong

The dream fades.

Uninvited Guest, Unexpected Gifts

CHAPTER ELEVEN

There she lay, back in her own bedroom: exhausted, stiff, sore, scarred, bruised, cut open and sewn back together again, handicapped, barely able to move her left arm and, primarily, alone with plenty of time and space to think. Most of the time her eyes were closed, drifting in and out of sleep. When her eyes were open, she saw the two get-better-soon-cards on the little bedside table. Evidently, some cared enough to have bought, written and sent them.

Both implied the same thing: recovery and the wish of the sender for that to occur soon. Was it cynicism? Was it irony? She couldn't get her tired head around which of the two words applied to her frame of mind. A mindset, which was unable to believe the message and which was unable to comprehend her chance of recovery.

Why would she recover? Did she deserve to get better? There were literally millions of people facing the same

predicament walking the earth's surface. The vast majority
were on their way to death, a certain and cruel death like
Mum's had been. Images of her mum's months of suffering
kept dragging her into shivers of repulsion that a similar
grossness was now being prepared inside her own body. She
couldn't find words harsh enough to describe what lay ahead
most likely. Prior to the operation, she had read up about
cancer, about treatments, about life expectancy, etcetera.
Although the statistics improved, most patients still died.
Especially the ones who had attracted secondary cancer were
doomed, with only a very, very rare exception.

Okay, she didn't belong to that category, at least not yet. In
the first place she would need to survive the present onslaught.
In the unlikely event she was one of those privileged, statistics
showed that survivors of primary cancer showed a high risk to
attract the illness a second time, like the modern day version
of stay of execution. What a prospect she faced. Basically, she
was struggling to survive, to beat the cancer, so as to continue
on the torturous road to a certain and cruel death, still due to
cancer. Indeed, what a prospect. So, why bother? These two
words kept following her: why bother?

There was a lot to think about, lying there all on her own,
often unable to fall asleep.

The oncologist had been enthusiastic when he had lowered
himself to speak to her directly after the operation, only the
once. He had stated clearly that all had gone according to plan
and that lesser mortals would make sure she received all the
care and attention required. Obviously, he had not used this
terminology, but his patronising mannerism, standing tall and
thin at her feet, had prompted her mind to conjure up this
variation. He wore dark-rimmed glasses, but a monocle would
have suited his superior attitude aptly.

Her mind's twists and turns took her by surprise more often
these days. They developed into her biggest source of
entertainment, coming up with the most crooked and morbid
statements, which made her snigger inwardly. No way did she

dare utter any of her sarcasms.

From the thin height of his ivory tower, he had updated her in a few sentences.

"Congratulations are in place. The operation went as smoothly as could have been expected. We traced the malignancy and removed it in no time at all. As a precautionary measure, the adjacent lymph nodes have been taken care off in similar fashion. They will undergo laboratory checks to determine any possible malignancies in their tissues. As soon as results are available, your GP shall be informed. He'll then invite you for a consultation."

"My GP is a woman."

"I apologise. That fact shall not affect procedures. I wish you a speedy recovery."

The rotation of his body looked like a series of movements aiming to prevent capsizing. He had disappeared without any further ado and had left her wondering.

"Adjacent lymph nodes had been taken care off in similar fashion" had been his exact words. Did that imply that they had also been removed? And if so, without her consent and without having first determined whether they'd actually been diseased or still totally healthy and functioning? The surgeon's visit had added concerns and questions to an already puzzled mind.

The nurse on duty had not been able to shed any light on the matter. The woman had no direct access to the patients' medical files, other than the ones concerning the necessary daily individual schedules and routines. She had advised the patient not to worry unduly, for the oncologist, together with his theatre staff, only had her best interest at heart, obviously. And in no time at all, to be totally frank with her, she would be allowed back home, receive reassurances and post-operative care from her GP and life would continue as if nothing untoward had ever happened. She'd be reunited with family and friends and would find herself back at work sooner rather than later.

Why was it that she mistrusted people who added the phrases "to be honest or frank" or "to be honest or frank with you" or, even worse, "to be totally honest or frank with you" after almost every sentence? Had Toni Blair instilled that mistrust in her? He had a habit of adding one of these phrases, using the variety "frank" predictably often. It had resulted in a movement aiming to have him face trial in The Hague for war crimes due to the illegal Iraq invasion, shoulder to shoulder with George W. Bush Jr. That protest movement had come to nothing of course, because protests rarely did.

A funny mind was growing inside her brain. Where did such a criticising attitude appear from, because when push came to shove, she was not in the least interested in politics. Was it a sign of a gradually advancing mistrust in life now that she couldn't even trust her own body any longer?

Even the tiniest amount of information the nurse could provide, felt worthless due to the woman's use of vocabulary. Also, the suggestion to seek advice and support from a MacMillan nurse seemed implausible in itself.

To her knowledge, however, the organisation was associated with support during terminal care as had been the case with mum. When she'd asked that nurse for more details, a series of denials and reassurances had been interwoven with those highly irritating quips, which were meant to instil trust, but which had the opposite effect entirely.

To be honest with her, one of her colleague-patients had attended a meeting at the Maggie's Centre, yet another support organisation, apparently with their own building on the hospital grounds somewhere. He'd known nothing in particular about the organisation, but he swore by the simple set-up and the inside knowledge of the group leader. What had really done it for him, were the stories of other people. Total strangers had shared their innermost intimate fears, doubts, insecurities and what not. He himself had also shared. A bit like Facebook, but then with all friends physically present. It had been scary. Once he had spoken, he'd felt proud as a peacock and had felt better for it. Everyone had listened intently and some had paid him compliments afterwards. Nobody had asked any tricky questions or ridiculed him in any way.

When she'd asked a different nurse about Maggie's, she'd been told it to be some Scottish initiative, started off by a man in commemoration of his late wife. Meetings were held on a daily basis at ten thirty, were free of charge and totally voluntary.

Why not try it out, she'd mused. An exploratory visit couldn't do any harm and if it wasn't her cup of tea, she could just leave and not come back.

Therefore, that next day, still weak, in pain and jittery, she had ventured direction Maggie's. Long corridors and elevators down to ground floor, more endless corridors and then through the garden towards a curiously designed building, had made the walk seem like the most treacherous journey ever undertaken. The closer she'd come, the more scepticism had increased, fuelled by the way she'd been treated and later, to put it bluntly, practically had been avoided by Dominique and Gwyneth. "Was she in the process of setting herself up once more for a bout of disappointment and disillusion?" her thoughts had cautioned. And why, why would she put herself through yet another trial in order to fail again most likely? The thoughts had slowed down her walking pace even further.

And when she'd come to a virtual standstill, a woman had exited the building, had introduced herself as Diana and had welcomed her inside, giving a supporting arm. Diana had cheerfully rattled away, that she could come and go as she pleased, that sharing or asking questions was not in the least mandatory, but totally up to the participants.

She'd been taken by surprise about the woman's happiness. She couldn't imagine herself like that if the cancer did vanish with the danger of a second attack looming over her in the distance. It didn't seem to bother the other woman, but then, had she had cancer? Wouldn't it be way too intrusive to ask?

She might be embarrassed like hell and most likely would despise to be reminded of the disease and leave the horror story behind her asap, once and for all. But then, Diana chose to work here, in the lion's den so to speak.

It was as if the other had read her mind and answered the unasked question.

"A few years ago I had cancer. The left breast has been removed. It's been quite something to get used to."

"If you don't mind me asking, are you not scared the cancer will return? I dread the possibility. If I survive this episode at all."

"No, I'm not. If it does, it does and we'll deal with. In the meantime, I've got much to be grateful for. Every time I see myself in the mirror or when I take a bath or a shower, I'm reminded of having had cancer. There's no denying that with only one breast remaining. But hey, what's one breast when the rest of me is healthy, healthier and happier than previously, actually. Would you like a cuppa?"

She would.

"Sugar, milk? There you go. Just take a seat. Take your pick and we'll start soon. Thank you for coming along. Today is not our usual meeting. We've got a speaker, who may be arriving any minute. By the way, what's your name?"

Her mouth opened to reply.

Diana, squeezing her right shoulder, stopped her in her tracks before a sound had been emitted and rushed off, apologetically, to welcome an elderly man in suit, shirt, tie and immaculately polished shoes. That was the speaker, no doubt.

She eyed the room.

Another woman scurried about, adjusting chairs around the coffee table, puffing up cushions, readying drinking glasses and filling water jugs. The concentration left her no time or space to divert attention away from the tasks in hand.

She sat down or, better, she sank down into a sofa, from which she'd never get up again without anybody's helping hand. The unexpected sinking made her spill some tea over her trousers. She had just put them on clean, she thought, annoyed. The sudden movement also painfully jerked her left armpit. A gasp of agony could only just be prevented. It made her want to leave, but she couldn't, imprisoned in the comfort of cushions and sofa.

In the end, eleven people gathered, including both women on duty and the official looking man.

Diana had welcomed them with saying that today's meeting was different from all other ones. There was not going to be the usual sharing of stories, but she had the indescribable honour to welcome the very man who was in the position of overseeing the establishment of new Maggie's centres all over the British Isles and possibly beyond. Diana had bowed like a penknife when putting him in the limelight.

She'd wanted stories. She'd wanted support. She'd wanted to tell her own story. She'd wanted them to help her get over her fear of telling her story. She had not dragged her body all this way for immaculately polished shoes and an ego to match. The carry on had made her feel uncomfortable and fidgety. All she'd wanted to do, was leave. For that, she would need help and ask for help and draw attention to herself. She'd hesitated, weighed up pros and cons and after some ten minutes had decided, "sod it" and had excused herself with a white lie of needing to spend a penny.

Diana had pulled her up by her healthy arm and had apologised profusely, as she had worded it, for today not being the regular kind of meeting and expected to see her again the next day, same time same place when all would be back to normal.

Her cynical mind commented silently: "My life will never be back to normal again. Nor will yours be, however strongly you all try to deny this naked fact by sticking your heads in the sand."

She had promised to return, knowing full well that she had no intention of doing so.

Back home alone, there was so much, such an unfathomable

lot to think about, lying all alone in her own bed, often unable to fall asleep.

The topic second in frequency to occupy her mind, was that weird dream. She rarely dreamt and when, she remembered dreams only infrequently. The sheer weirdness had stunned her into disbelief and she brought her own sanity into doubt. It had been the first time that she'd been curious about its interpretation.

She had googled some American dream interpretation website and had transferred the hundred fifty dollar. Literally within two minutes a reply had been received. The first two pages had been filled with welcoming her unique request ever so over the top enthusiastically, whilst slipping into hardcore marketing within the same initial paragraph. The explanation of her dream itself took no more than two short paragraphs, followed by the urgent invitation to sign up for their weekly newsletter and, even more recommendable, to attend their week long dream retreat in Mount Shasta, California. After that, her inbox had been inundated with aggressive junk mail until she had unsubscribed. The latter she'd to do three times.

Both relevant paragraphs had told only blablabla bullshit about the sacredness of her being, of her soul, of her spiritual path and that she doubtlessly had received a strong calling to step boldly into her healership, aligning physical incarnation with her soul's direction during this life time. None of the factual dream symbols, like woods, birch trees, deer or unicorn had been specifically referred to, let alone explained. It was all a big new age con, she had concluded, for which she had been stupid and naïve enough to fork out about one hundred quid, but, never again.

That initiative had made her none the wiser and had most definitely not satisfied her deep intrigue about a quite incredible piece of coincidence. Unicorns were an unknown quantity to her and their mythological significance a total mystery. To her knowledge she hadn't come across unicorns before in any shape or form and suddenly twice in the space of a few months.

The first encounter had occurred several months ago, when she had dipped her toe into the world of new age by playing that board game. Once she had been born, so-called, the group leader had asked her to pick a white card from a little envelope. He described them as "Angel Cards". Each of these card had depicted an angel and one word, typifying a certain quality the receiver was invited to focus on or feel supported by during the game weekend. There'd been angels of Love, Light, Harmony, Synthesis and many more. All in all well over fifty of them.

Her angel had been "Trust". Pretty good, like all of them had been pretty good, albeit sticky sweet really.

Amazing and hard to comprehend, was, that the drawing on her card was that of a winged angel, kneeling in front of a unicorn. And then, months later, she'd dreamt exactly that particular image. She couldn't get her head around it and that American company had categorically failed to shed any light on the matter and had attempted to lure her into spending more money. And she, stupid and gullible cow that she was, had naively fallen for the temptation.

Back home, there was a lot to think about, lying all alone in her own bed, often unable to fall asleep.

Her dad had brought her to the hospital. As agreed, she had informed him of the appointment as soon as the letter had arrived and he'd cleared his diary for her sake. During that first phone call and when they were driving there and in the waiting room, he had repeated how it was solely for her benefit that he was accompanying her. A meeting with a loyal customer of decades had had to be postponed, which had been a first with the exception of when his wife, her mum had been ill. Customers and their requirements deserve preference over anything else, was one of his main business slogans. Decades of prolonged success of the enterprise was proof that the philosophy worked. In the end, the business had provided well for the family.

How often had she not heard that sermon? Did he want her to feel guilty at all cost?

How guilty had he made her mum feel, come to think of it, dragging her husband away from his work, his baby and income providing duty? How often had she herself not been forced to reconsider her own wishes and needs and had sacrificed them, for the sake of ...

For the sake of what exactly? For the sake of family security, his career, his ego? And, what had been sacrificed? Harmony at home, health, his own wife? Her mind boggled.

He had been unnaturally chatty, when picking her up. During the drive, his chattiness had become somewhat forced. When parking and walking from the parking lot to and then through the main entrance, his chattiness had turned into a strained, incoherent kind of babble. From his normally erect posture, his physique had changed into that of a burdened man. From her front door to the hospital's main entrance, her father had aged twenty years, from young mid fifties and in the full flow of life to ashen grey and burdened, suffering.

The buoyant fifty plus year old man could have acted as a rock for his daughter. The ashen grey man in his seventies, she didn't dare trouble. Memories haunted him, obviously, but why couldn't he put his stuff on the back burner for only a few hours for once? It hadn't been fitting, under present circumstances highly inappropriate even, for him to take centre stage in needily seeking attention. She'd kept quiet though.

No sooner had father and daughter stepped through the automatic doors, wide enough for two stretchers, then he had regressed.

"It all looks the same still, more or less. Nothing much has changed. Don't know how often I've wheeled your mother along this corridor and brought her outside for a breath of fresh air. She enjoyed that. It was one of the last things I could do for her. And I did it, almost every day. And then we went here....."

Uninvited Guest, Unexpected Gifts

He had, surprisingly, gone ahead and taken his daughter on a tour.

Not that she'd needed it. Also for her the place symbolised a shockingly painful memory lane, overshadowed however by the present situation, which he had appeared to disregard. The last thing she'd wanted, was to be shown around and be relegated to third place, behind, now, both parents' needs.

Gesturing as if the café belonged to his own emporium, he had pointed out their regular window table (as if she didn't remember), told how he had ordered a large cappuccino and millionaires shortbread (as if she didn't remember) and how her mother had enjoyed seeing him eating and drinking, also when she had no longer been capable of swallowing or digesting or tasting any morsel and had been drip-fed intravenously (as if she didn't remember). He'd had to be pulled away from the place.

No sooner had they left the café and entered the maze of signs, corridors, elevators, wards and waiting rooms, then he'd fallen silent. Barely a word had left his lips before she'd been summoned.

He had stood in front of her. Shovels of hands had grabbed her right one. All he had been able to whisper, was that he would be back later that evening. His fingers held her hand in a bone crushing grip.

His goodbye had been devastatingly painful for her. For the first time after Charlie's arrival, he'd allowed her to witness the depth of his still lingering heart ache. It had torn his daughter's heart agonisingly apart and had squeezed the phalanges of her right hand close to breaking point. The hand had hurt for days. As if he had forced her to carry his grief into the operating theatre for her as focal point in stead of the sharp, post-operative pains after waking up again.

What about her own pains? What about her own fear? What about her deep existential insecurities? These questions had been whispered, but only unobtrusively soft, so as not to interfere with the agony he had shouldered for almost a decade and still shouldered and had imprinted into his daughter's hand.

That had been the only time he'd been alone with his daughter in hospital. Had he not dared a solo follow-up, because from then on the only function of his physical presence had appeared the reiteration to imprint his agony into her right hand. The rest of him had seemed absent.

Had Charlie's dominance demanded the upper hand? Whatever the reason, visiting times had been a threesome affair with father's girlfriend holding the reigns. She had also accompanied the stepdaughter back home, together with a carload of previously purchased and unasked for necessities. There'd been some genuinely necessary items, like basic foods and some utterly useless ones, like gossipy magazines, she never normally glanced at.

Back home, there was a lot to think about, lying all alone in her own bed, often unable to fall asleep.

Two "Get Better Soon" cards stood spread open on the bedside table. Each gave her a lot to think about and not the gratitude about somebody's attentive gesture, but a sourish cynicism.

One card depicted a smiling bear giving it the thumbs up with a bandage wrapped around the thumb. It had come from the bank with written inside solely the text: "from all of us at work" without individual names of her colleagues or any further specifics. How impersonal could it get and that after almost a decade of dedication day after day. She had known some of these people all this time and they had known her just as long, naturally. The three pounds, including the stamp, would have been paid out of the metallic blue petty cash box and someone would have gone out of her way during lunchtime to buy the cheerful thing. Whether Dominique had informed the others of the seriousness of her illness, she didn't know of course. He might not have out of ethical confidentiality. But, then again, he might have and if he'd done so, the lack of impersonal touch stung even deeper.

Uninvited Guest, Unexpected Gifts

The second card showed a hunk of a male nurse rushing a stretcher in full speed around a bend from a hospital to a house with the word "Home" written on it, whilst the sexy blond patient was holding on for dear life with big boobs just not escaping from a red lacy bra. The choir had sent it with the text "Hope you will be with us soon again" and had added in tiny letters "admin is piling up". All of it was meant to be taken with a pinch of salt and in good humour, naturally. It didn't feel humorous to her. Especially the patient's big healthy and sexy pair of breasts hurt and made her want to throw up. Clear was, that Gwyneth had not informed the choir members of the details of her illness, for if she had done, the card turned into the epitome of a sick joke. However, the small letters did reek of exactly that. As if her administrative efforts had been her only worth these last years.

Yes, it was nice that they had thought of her at the bank and in the choir, but warmth or comfort they had failed to ignite in her. It all seemed nothing more than just the right thing to do.

Back home, there was a lot to think about, lying all alone in her own bed, often unable to fall asleep.

Three days she'd been home now and most of it had been spent in bed. She slept when sleep arrived. She read a novel she'd read twice before. She watched some TV. She listened to some CD's she knew by heart. She finger-tipped her breast underneath the dressing. She looked forward to the district nurse coming in the morning to change it, not the breast, but the dressing. She smiled each time at her own play of words, pleased she as she was to be still capable of the tiniest of jokes and capable of smiling. She caressed the healthy breast often, asking it to remain healthy and give the diseased one the right example as well as encouragement. She moved and stretched and lifted her left arm as instructed, tentatively. Each day a tiny bit more movement was evident, causing a smidgen less pain. She was on the mend. She repeated the short sentence frequently, for the concept of mending to replace the negative thought of the previously terminal illness and to replace her father's burdensome imprint into the bones of her hand. She thought that shift in mindset a peculiar idea, but something had ignited the initiative in her mind and made her continue.

She was on the mend.

The short, five word sentence gave her a boost, a much needed boost after weeks of turbulence. It implied that her body was recovering on its own accord without chemotherapy. Six doses had been scheduled with three week intervals.

That, according to the oncologist, gave the best rate of recovery with the smallest possible chance of a relapse, although nothing could be guaranteed. Matter of factly, six dates and six time slots had been set aside.

Due to the normality of standard procedures, she had not been given any option to refuse if that would have been her wish, which it wasn't obviously. All she wished for, was for cancer to be gone out of her life and gone forever. If chemo was going to contribute to that, she only ought to be grateful for the advance in medical science.

Her mum had had chemo and lots of it, as well as high doses of radiotherapy. It had been reiterated time and time again, how medical procedures had prolonged her life. Mum's quality of life had suffered, for sure, but it had been extended by at least half a year, which had been something to be grateful for and to treasure, oncologist, GP and nurses had pointed out to her and her father.

Mum's cancer had been detected at a much later stage. Precautionary scanning had not yet been invented by then.

Hers was caught much earlier and she'd been operated on much sooner and the chemo she almost looked forward to as a next step towards full recovery. Besides that, without chemotherapy her body was already on the mend.

Uninvited Guest, Unexpected Gifts

CHAPTER TWELVE

She was devastated.

Nine weeks had gone by after the operation and everything went according to schedule. She had received two bouts of chemo.

Yes, she'd looked forward to the six treatments as these all important steps towards leaving cancer in the past, as an episode in her life, which had been scary, which had been filled with a troubled mind, some sleepless nights, a bit too much alcohol and too many sleeping tablets. However, the episode had not gotten the better of her either. She had taken the all important steps towards resuming a normal life again and was well on her way.

And yes, she had witnessed the effect chemotherapy had had on her mum, but science had advanced tremendously. And yes, the oncologist and the GP had made her aware of the possible side effects. Besides that, she knew all about the horror stories from newspapers, TV, magazines and the like. It wouldn't get her down, though. Now that she was on the mend again, her body had shown its resilience. It could be trusted after all, also in dealing with chemo without any significant mishaps.

Faith in her physique had replaced the previously domineering fear and had provided nights filled with sound and dreamless sleep.

The scars faded. Besides, they'd only been small to start with. The larger one underneath her armpit, where the lymph nodes had been removed, was invisible unless she lifted her arm really high up. So, nobody would notice. The one on the side of her breast was minuscule and also healed rapidly. The district nurse had said something very encouraging on several occasions:

"Your body is still young and heals well."

Outwardly she had not reacted to the remarks, but could have embraced the woman, could have kissed her and could have thanked her on her bare knees. The nurse's sentence lingered and fed the already increasing trust in her healing capacities. Maybe there was still hope that a man would desire her and even desire her breasts after all of this was finished.

Her arm movements were virtually back to normal and only still caused minor discomfort during certain sudden movements.

Bags of money she was not able to lift yet. For that, somebody's assistance had to be called upon, which felt a bit awkward. Otherwise, everybody had welcomed her warmly back at work. Even Dominique had reacted friendlier than usual and he seemed genuinely pleased to have her back and not just because one colleague was on holiday and another had been on sick leave for over a fortnight with an attack of sciatica (ironically enough, due to lifting those heavy bags of coins). Yes he did seem genuinely pleased to have her back, because on the first day back at work, he'd spent nigh on quarter of an hour, asking some details, encouraging her not to overdo things and inviting her to ask for support if and when required. On leaving his office, she'd been inwardly glowing.

Choir practise had resumed. The practise itself had been awesome, just awesome and made her realise how much she'd missed singing. Not much time and not many words had been spent on welcoming her back, although, Gwyneth had even hugged her with the briefest of embraces. The low key reunion had been forgotten as soon as they'd started rehearsing Beethoven's Ninth. She'd sung her parts like she'd never sung before, except maybe when in duet with that chaffinch, almost thirty years ago. That had been different kettle of fish altogether.

Somebody had filmed and recorded the entire piece, without her having been aware of it. All others had been in the know, but had forgotten to inform her and afterwards all of them had gathered around the laptop to watch the result.

"Ode to Joy" had been her first song after weeks of illness. The title had always tickled and inspired her as well as the lyrics of the entire composition, especially its first verse:

O Freunde, nicht diese Tone!
Sondern lasst uns angenehmere anstimmen
und freudenvollere!

The English translation, included in the box set with all nine symphonies, which had been part of her extensive classical collection, was as follows:

O friends, no more these sounds!
Let us sing more cheerful songs,
More full of joy!

This time even more so. She'd sung her heart and lungs out in one eighteen minute long celebration of life and its divine origins. Joined in joy with her co-performers, there'd been no holding her back. She remembered how she had experienced the entire event in full awareness: the ecstasy, the thrill, the exquisiteness of the composition. The main thrill, though, had been the fact of her being able to perform once more amidst the other members. She had envisaged the performance to revitalise every cell of her breast and lymph nodes. Singing in general was going to contribute to her healing, especially the singing of this particular ode. She'd convinced herself of that.

And then to realise, that Beethoven, the master himself, had never heard the piece, deaf as he had been at the time of its first public performance. Whilst conducting, as goes the story, he had, on occasion, tried to catch a glimpse of the audience behind him to get an impression whether they appreciated it or not, revolutionary unique as the composition had been at the time of writing.

There they had sat and stood, the entire choir, her choir, all gathered around the laptop.

It had made her self-conscious to the extreme, already beforehand. The idea alone of being watched, recorded, for all and sundry to see her perform, horrified her.

The troupe had watched themselves and each other critically. They had listened, equally critically.

None of the critique, positive as well as negative, had reached her. All she'd noticed, was her mouth agape and the first sentence popping up in her mind had been: "Grandmother, what a big mouth you've got." That scene from Little Red Riding Hood had frightened her witless as a girl. How a wolf could disguise himself as a grandmother to fool that sweet, innocent girl. It had taken a lot of persuasion from all adults to get her to regain trust in all four grandparents.

She'd paid no attention to any of the others. The actual singing she'd failed to register. The only feature she'd seen, was that huge hole, where her entire face had seemed to disappear into. There'd been no tongue or teeth visible. Only that empty cavity above a stretched, elongated throat, whilst the head kept veering backwards.

And when somebody had commented on her silence, she'd simply stated to have been awestruck.

Uninvited Guest, Unexpected Gifts

True as her reply had been, the harsh truth she would never admit to anyone. To admit it to herself had been bad enough. She'd berated herself for days and promised to behave according to her age next time. The excuse of a liberating and exhilarating first singing experience after a possibly life threatening illness, compensated only to a certain extent. Still, the images of self-ridicule kept following her.

And when one of the guys, she couldn't even remember who, had asked if anyone would like a copy to take home the following week, all had reacted enthusiastically.

She'd declined.

Gwyneth had taken it upon herself to monitor the admin side of things during her absence and had asked her, on leaving, if she could have a word. That had been the exact expression used. Firstly, Gwyneth had brushed the previous two troublesome months aside with some deadpan remarks, that she knew for certain that the illness had been beaten and that life would resume as usual in no time at all.

She hadn't responded.

On closer investigation, Gwyneth had used the very right expression. She'd monitored the administration and nothing else. Some print-outs of e-mails had been handed over, together with two sheets of almost illegible scribbles of names and phone numbers. They concerned four people, including one man (and men they were in desperate need of, Gwyneth had added with a twinkling innuendo in her eyes), who wished to join the choir. Could she please give them a call and check whether they were suitable? Hastily, the four phone numbers and e-mail addresses had been pointed out to her. Furthermore, the rent for their rehearsal studio was due. A reminder had already been received and Gwyneth had waved a sheet of paper through the air. Could she please pay the bill asap? Also, two organisations had requested them to perform, which resulted in the waving about of two more sheets. Could she please check both, set preliminary dates and bring further details along next time? The group had decided to join an X-

Factor kind of contest with 'Ode to Joy'. Could she please request an application form?

Automatically she had agreed, bamboozled by what had landed on her lap. Then they'd left and said their goodbyes when she had entered her tube station.

Gwyneth lived only two streets away.

Crammed in the underground, nausea had welled up and once she'd returned home, she'd briefly leafed through the paperwork. Some of the e-mails had been over a month old and needed seeing to sooner rather than later. She'd poured herself a generous g&t, the first drink after having been discharged from hospital and had slept badly that night.

By then she had received chemotherapy twice. Her body dealt with the onslaught above expectation and all warnings about disastrous side effects seemed strongly exaggerated.

That next day the third one was due. Dominique had allowed her a full day off each time, which felt very generous, because appointments had been scheduled as early in the morning as possible to have the rest of the day to recover. She wanted them over and done with. She wanted the cancer episode to be over and done with. She wanted those days to be over and done with and embrace a life, a future without hospital visits.

Each time after chemo, once she left the compound and stepped onto the pavement, she brushed her hair. It had grown into a ritual. As if the human touch brushed off the typical hospital smell and atmosphere.

She liked her hair and always had done. It was full with a healthy shine, blond, waving over her shoulders. She looked after it well and followed her hairdresser's recommendations to the letter.

That next day, after that third chemo, she stepped onto the pavement, very deliberately taking a giant step from the one realm into the next. She turned around, smiled and in her mind ticked off the third appointment in a series of six. She was halfway there, which felt like a turning point. From this moment on, counting down replaced adding up and that implied that the finishing line came in sight. She'd reached the final straight, so to speak. The smile continued when she fished the hairbrush out of her handbag and enjoyed how the brush glided effortlessly through her blond lusciousness, several times. On these occasions she loved to apply slightly more pressure to massage the scalp simultaneously. It felt like the right thing to do, the scratching stimulating her circulation. The sensation brought her back to her own true self, it seemed, owning herself again, whereas in hospital, she felt owned by others, by medication, by equipment.

As usual her other hand removed loose hairs from the brush before placing it back into the handbag.

There were not a few loose hairs. There was a tuft, an entire tuft, almost a fistful.

She looked at her hand and the smile vanished when reality dawned and hit her like a ton of bricks. Her hair. Her lovely, treasured hair was falling out. That horrid and well known side effect of chemotherapy arrived and she had done so well to escape such calamities. Well, no longer. She too fell victim.

She was devastated.

She looked at the ugly, ugly building, wanted to run back inside and demand of them to undo this, show them what they had done to her beautiful hair, give them proof of their horrendous so-called health care and tell them the truth of what she really felt. She clenched her fist, the one with the tuft and stuffed it deep, deep into her coat pocket. She wanted to scream and didn't, couldn't. It was too public a location. She would make a right fool of herself or, worse, might get arrested for public disorder.

She was devastated.

What to do? Where to go? Home. Where else? But, her chin trembled. An emotional outburst was imminent. Travelling home on the underground, squeezed together with hundreds of strangers, wandering through four different tube stations. And all of that sobbing? No way. Take a bus? One wouldn't suffice. She counted on her fingers, the free fingers which had earlier held the hairbrush, that she would need to take an equal number of buses, possibly one more even. Out of the question.

The taxi set her back twenty quid and during the entire journey she cried buckets.

The driver was worried, asked and was told in no uncertain terms to mind his own business. He did.

Uninvited Guest, Unexpected Gifts

CHAPTER THIRTEEN

The next morning, at the moment she awoke with an immobilised jolt, which was in fact nothing more than an awareness kicking in at full speed, she froze.

Sleep had been fitful and now, on waking, each finger felt heavy, barely able to move. Each toe ditto. Feet and hands carried a dead weight. It felt as if they had sunk deep, deep into the mattress overnight, unable to resurface. Not just feet and hands or toes and fingers, all of her was weighted down. The head, one of the heaviest part of human anatomy, felt lightest, or, least heavy. She turned her head to check the time. Five minutes before the alarm clock was going to activate Classic FM and she would need to rise.

Rise.

She tasted the word, because her brain functioned. It soon became heavy with thoughts, though. But, that didn't prevent movement. Heaviness of body did and when the radio started at exactly 07.30 that very same body had to move. It had to rise. It had to shower. It had to dress itself. It had to make a cup of tea and some toast, although, that it didn't have to do, but breakfast being the most important meal of the day, skipping it seemed a criminal act against tradition. See, the brain functioned. She smiled. Effortlessly, she noticed. A smile was effortless when all other bodily functions cost disproportionate amounts of effort.

When looking at the clock, her eyes had registered something else. That something else dawned in slow motion. As did the question, whether it was true what she thought to have caught a glimpse of. Everything happened in a forced slow motion, which seemed a trauma-activated slow motion, which made time stop, even though the red digits had progressed to 07.45.

Gradually, yesterday's disastrous happening outside the hospital returned to conscious memory. The pain she had experienced there and then and for the rest of that day as well as during the night, came back in full force. It made her not want to turn her head again. It made her want to lie still. It made her unwilling to be aware. It made her want to forget all of life and sink, sink, sink into oblivion. If it turned out to be true what she thought to have noticed.

Curiosity won the internal battle, for better or for worse and she dared. Happy as she had been previously, that her neck muscles obeyed her will pretty smoothly, she now felt trepidation filled with anxiety before and during the physical act of turning. The act seemed to take five minutes, but digits remained at 07.48 throughout the move.

When the motion had been completed, she froze further still and deep into the marrow of her bones, she chilled.

Between her eyes and the alarm clock, the pillow was covered in hair. Shock mobilised her hand without her actually realising the previous impossibility. Her hand searched for the truth and the truth finding mission took priority over her exhaustion. Somehow the body obeyed. Somehow, where it

94

had been unable to do so only twenty five minutes earlier. And when the hand showed her eyes its unwanted, despicable harvest, all five of her fingers closed into a tight fist and her eyes closed, shut tightly and her mouth grunted a moan, a long moan, a moan long enough to turn into a sob, a sob from the deepest caverns of her abdomen.

Yes, the brain functioned and functioned well. Nevertheless, at the moment of impact, it was unable to fathom all occurrences and consequences as well as coming up with fitting adjectives, expressions or swearwords even.

She was stunned, but then again, much more than just stunned. She was devastated, but then again much more than just the sum of stunned and devastated. She was exasperated, but then again much more than just the sum of stunned, devastated and exasperated. She was all of the above combined and so much more. So very, very much more, that also her brain appeared to become a dead weight, overloaded by experiences and emotions of darkness, encapsulating body as well as mind.

There she was lying, motionless and brain dead with a clenched fist full of hair.

Naturally, each popular middle of the road kind of music station knows how to catch the right mood at the right time, frequently programmed as such, frequently unbeknown to its DJ's and producers. Classic FM being, pardon the pun, a classic example.

Classic FM hit bull's eye with this particular listener. Nothing had been pre-arranged, but was pure coincidence or, as some would have it, a compassionate right-time-right-place act of the universe.

The eight o'clock news failed to register. Introductions and announcements beforehand and afterwards also fell on deaf ears. The initial notes and lines of the first composition were impactive in extremis, however. Her brain functioned optimally and remembered vividly the positive effect this particular composition had had just two days earlier.

Tjitze de Jong

She couldn't keep herself from singing. Initially, caution ruled and she sang subdued, because, was she able to sing and was she not overdoing it? Should she preserve her precious energy for the day ahead, once movement returned? Because when her physical movements would become easier, she planned to arrive at work just an hour or so later, apologise profusely, explain matters and they would understand hopefully. In the end, she had survived a cancer scare, or, at least, was in the process of surviving it. That did have to count for something.

She couldn't keep herself from singing each choral section of the full eighteen minutes worth of Beethoven's Ninth. There she lay, horizontal, barely able to move a limb and she sang. Not with the previous fervour of their joint choir practise, for that was impossible lying down, but she sang. About halfway she felt some weird kind of tingling in her arms and legs. The unfamiliar sensation frightened her to begin with, but she gave herself a talking to, berating initially and then encouraging. Afterwards she was unable to recall what had brought on that shift in self-approach. However, she was mighty glad she had persisted and not listened to her frightened inner voice of doom en gloom. The prickling extended into her fingers and toes and all twenty started to move on the bombastic rhythms. Her voice grew close to full volume towards the end and when the eighteen minutes were over, the pillow was soaked on either side of her head, as were her loosened hairs.

She could move. This most normal of human functions, locomotion, brought her to tears. Silly, she thought and then again, the shock had been very intense, not too intense for it to remain throughout Beethoven's Ninth, which was quite some realisation. She had cause for celebration. She was unsure about what and how, but she intended to treat herself to some different kind of breakfast.

Her torso raised off the mattress, only slightly more challenging than normal. The legs swung with relative ease over the side of the bed. Sitting upright caused no problem and

96

the expected dizziness didn't materialise. She felt victorious.

When aiming to push herself into a full vertical position, she became aware of her fist still clenching that tuft of hair in a vice-like grip. Her eyes drifted from hand to pillow and her other hand, her left one, stroked her hair carefully, afraid to run fingers through it for fear of causing more irreparable damage. Not many hairs, by no means a tuft, but most definitely more than could be expected under normal circumstances, glided through the air and landed softly on the duvet. They took their time. Not that she needed time to loose her notion of having conquered physical challenges. She fell back onto the bed, filled with a sense of loss, of having lost.

Classic FM added to her feeling disturbed and she switched it off. The clock said 08.45.

In fifteen minutes she ought to arrive at the bank which felt like an impossibility. Would she be capable of work at all? Maybe not, but, then, they were already short-staffed, she thought with a pang of guilt. After the fifteen minutes had passed, she would make up her mind, ring and tell them she'd be in after lunch and that she'd try and make up for lost time. In the meantime, she'd take it really easy, indulge in a long, hot bath, experiment with scarves to hide her vanishing hair, write some e-mails or make some phone calls for the choir and not embark on anything too energetically demanding.

The plan worked out. She rose, wrapped up in her dressing gown and tied the ribbon more securely than usual as if it would provide extra support. She rang the bank, was unable to get hold of Dominique and asked for the message to be passed on once his current meeting had finished. The steamy, foamy bath nourished her into deep relaxation. So much so, that exiting the tub felt like a chore and undid some of its benefits. The dressing gown rekindled and accentuated comfort. Tea and toast followed. The tea she took with sugar this time and she layered the toast thick with honey. Normally sweetness wasn't that appealing, but her body demanded comfort on all fronts.

Whilst chewing, she gathered her two scarves, the phone and Gwyneth's notes and print-outs. First finish breakfast, she thought and then try to get hold of these new membership applicants.

No sooner had she swallowed the last bite, then tiredness hit home. The choir's paperwork on the table, repulsed her. But, who else was going to take care of it? She'd agreed to both functions and was obliged to fulfil all necessary tasks, even with a slight aversion if need be. She sighed, picked up a sheet, read letters, words, sentences. None of it made sense and she put the paper back. She felt pathetic and her chin fell heavily into the V-shape of both hand palms.

What ailed her? Surely, this couldn't be the dreaded tiredness linked with chemo? She must have a cold or flu coming on or something less sinister creeping up on her. For, if it was induced by chemo, why only now after three treatments? Why not earlier, after the first or second session? Then again, it was also only now, after that blasted third session, that that horrid hair loss had started. So, maybe this was it, whilst she had coped so well. Her body had coped so well, that she had begun to think the side effects were going to pass her by. Well, dream on. This was it apparently and she better get used to another few weeks of the same or was worse to come? Another few weeks? No, it was more likely going to be a few months. There were three more chemo treatments planned at three weeks intervals and that made nine weeks and for the onslaught to leave her system totally, may well take another three weeks, adding up to twelve weeks, i.e. nigh well three months altogether. What an appalling prospect.

And what she experienced now was considered normal? This was what millions of people faced as a result of cancer and chemo? No wonder, she pondered, that the media paid much more attention to cancer than to any other illness, calling it the illness of illnesses or however the slogan went.

How was she able to work, to travel there and back as well as fulfil her duties? How could she deal with the choir admin?

Uninvited Guest, Unexpected Gifts

How could she shop, cook and clean?

Just as well she barely had any friends left. At least, she was not going to be a disappointment to them.

CHAPTER FOURTEEN

"Nine weeks of ongoing and relentless incapacitated hell", was how she had heard herself describe, what she had lived through. No, pain had barely played a role, at least not physically.

Emotionally it had been a horrendously taxing journey. In particular the ongoing humiliation on any conceivable front seemed to have slaughtered every single bit of self-esteem out of her. Self-esteem and confidence had never been her strongest point anyway and now, a pathetically exhausting helplessness had dumped her into constant dependency. The most menial tasks had drained her. First of all the prospect of having to perform a task had worried her to bits, no matter what, no matter how simple. And then, after long deliberation, actually doing it or attempting to in some sort of half-baked fashion.

She'd loathed her bothersome existence and the question of

who she actually had turned out to be, slowly demanded to be answered and she frequently found herself taking stock of her life.

She was the daughter of her parents, of whom her father was a rather successful businessman, employing about a hundred people. Her mum had died and she had copied her, except that she hadn't died yet. Yet. She was a simple cashier at a bank and as such easily replaceable. She was one of the two sopranos of a choir as well as their administrative coordinator. As the former not that easily replaceable. As the latter easy-peasy, except for the fact that none of the others could be bothered to replace her even if only temporarily.

All in all, her existence added up to a pretty meagre score after living some thirty plus years. This final conclusion didn't deliver any positive contribution to her state of mind whatsoever and only deepened gloominess. She tried not to visit the subject again and attempted to remain focused on practicalities, of which there were plenty to get to grips with. But she couldn't prevent her mind from wandering, similar to her fingertips right at the beginning of this episode, ages ago now. She'd also been unable to prevent them from wandering back to the lump time and time again.

Groceries were being delivered and carried inside. Waitrose, her regular supermarket, didn't offer a delivery service. As a result, she had tried out the other three, in alphabetical order: ASDA, Sainsbury's and TESCO. Their assortment was not nearly as satisfactory in quality as her usual produce from Waitrose and it didn't motivate her to prepare proper meals, if energy allowed, which was rarely the case.

Gradually she had to succumb to the fact, that cooking was being reduced to microwaving ready-made meals and sticking pizzas in the oven.

Or, alternatively and worst of all, Charlie had been so kind to prepare meals for her. Stepmum had pointed out, that she only needed to call her and say what she liked to eat that day. Like a private delivery service. Could it be made any easier for her and no, honest, it was no problem at all, the woman had offered ever so kindly. Could she please allow her to look after her partner's daughter for once? The generosity of spirit was undermined by the habitual little guilt imposing quips. Subtly hours and miles were brought into the equation, contradicting the no-problem-at-all-offer and changing the voluntary acts of unconditional kindness into acts of self-imposed martyrdom.

Stepdaughter hated the entire circus of pretence. Why did her father have to have a new girlfriend and why, for heaven's sake, had he chosen this one? Her dislike for the woman increased by the day. Still, under present circumstances, did she have a choice in the matter? Not really. The only option left, was to grin and bear it, keep quiet and say "Thank you" as if she meant it.

Her father visited Sundays, always in company, naturally. Their conversations were limited to platitudes, empty, meaningless and when she got the impression that emphasising her stepmum's generous and sacrificial share in her recovery was of greater significance than the possibility of recovery itself, daughter started to dread Sundays. Traditional Sunday roast with all the trimmings had always been her favourite meal of the week. Even that lost its appeal, spoiled by reduced appetite, by forced gratitude, by the cook's personality and, above all, by it being reheated, because it had to be prepared in father's mod con giant kitchen. Her own tiny and limited space and equipment would never do. That message was brought home. Ever so subtly, obviously.

Baldness, knackered and loss of appetite, these were the three most common side effects of chemo and she suffered them all, full on. During the week she could live her own rhythm, please herself and eat what and when she wished, if at all. Most days it came to very little. A few mouthfuls of pizza, for example and the rest went in the bin, for chewing took too much effort. A tin of soup, no matter which flavour, looked ever so appetising, but after several spoonfuls, aversion kicked in and the rest was poured down the sink. Occasional biscuits or toast thick with butter and honey became staple diet.

As a result, she lost weight. She didn't notice, but Charlie commented on it and increased her culinary efforts. At some point, the woman, for want of a more rude word, had taken it upon herself to investigate the bin. Once Charlie had detected how much of her food, prepared ever so lovingly and which had taken hours of her precious time, was going to waste, a lecture had followed.

Of course father had joined in. He'd sat right diagonally in front of his daughter and Charlie left diagonally.

When comments kept coming, memories of her once in a lifetime Wimbledon men's final with Federer life on centre court surfaced. Left to right, right to left, left to right her head had moved. Until dizziness had set in, when she'd been forced to shut her eyes and steady herself. Apologising for tiredness getting the better of her, she had got up and lay down.

All of the Sunday roast had gone to waste and that had been rubbed in well and truly, albeit, disguised by phrases of how 'understandable considering present circumstances' and 'would she like some on a plate covered with cling film to microwave later?' and 'by all means rest and I shall tidy op your kitchenette for you'. The woman actually always referred to her kitchen as 'kitchenette'.

Her brain kept functioning perfectly and over the weeks she invented the nickname: "The queen of subtle insults" for Charlie.

The damage had been done. From that Sunday onwards on a daily basis, she cast her eyes over her torso, pained by the fact she was able to count her ribs, solely by looking. Yet another reason to feel depressed. As if she needed more reasons. She felt depressed the way it was.

When she was not horizontal in bed, she often sat in front of the window. It was a big window on the eighth and top floor, one of the features she'd felt drawn to and the view had been strongly emphasised on the estate agent's website, in its brochure and during her initial viewing. True as it was, for the rest it was a pretty bog standard flat for a single person, typically one to give young people a start on the property ladder.

Her father had insisted on her purchasing something more extravagant in a more upmarket neighbourhood. When she'd protested that she would never be able to afford the monthly payments, he'd offered to buy a suitable property for her and then she could repay the loan as slowly as she wished. She had refused, but had remained unable to prevent him from buying this one for her on a similar condition. Of course, it made life easier and the flat would never run the chance of being repossessed by the bank. Because, her income was steady, but lowish and being employed by a bank and mortgage provider provided no added security whatsoever. A financial agreement remained a financial agreement and no advantages were to be expected.

The arrangement was safe. Too safe for her liking. Whereas the safety aspect itself she could live with and, honestly, felt like a bonus, but what nagged, was the fact that her father had also created a financial tie with his daughter, as if she was unable to provide security for herself, as if she remained dependent on her dad to a certain extent even at the ripe old age of thirty five.

That on its own also wasn't that bad either, but he had explained the situation to Charlie and that woman didn't miss an opportunity to drop the occasional hint into conversations. The term 'sugar daddy' had not been mentioned as such, but it wasn't far off.

Yes, the view was incredible from high up, overlooking the city with the London Eye rotating in the hazy distance and the high rises of the financial district adjacent. There was life. There was movement. There were commuters as she had been and maybe would be again one day. There was traffic flowing most of the time and jammed at other times. A bit like her own life, which had been flowing happily and freely for years and was now at a virtual standstill.

That standstill life of the present knew one location only: her flat. The four walls of her flat had become her verticalised horizon. Her world had been reduced to one flat and one flat only and a rather small one for that. She experienced moments of wanting to scream, to run to the elevator, zoom down and run through the street, her street, which seemed her street no longer, imprisoned as she had become. Not unlike that princess in the tower waiting to be rescued by a prince on a white horse. No, not in the least like that princess, for the princess had had long flowing, strong hair, which she had draped out of the window. The image had caught her imagination as a girl. Now it hurt.

Even the few trees made her envious now, whereas she had pitied them previously, asphalted into the pavement, surrounded by only a circle of soil not wider than ten centimetres around the stem. The asphalt left little space for rainwater to drain into the earth and for the roots to absorb nutrition. Leaves were sparse and never looked truly healthy, not even when they were still fresh and young in Spring. In comparison, each tree had a far freer existence than herself at present. They could stand outside in sun and rain and wind, which ruffled the leaves playfully. How long ago was it, that she had felt the wind through her hair. Hair? Which hair?

Whatever her eyes focused on, her mind came up with comparisons and continuously she came off worse.

Not a single squeak she'd heard from either bank or choir, except for Gwyneth popping in to collect her own paperwork. The other choir members had sent their regards. Nothing else had been forthcoming from either source during the entire three months. Being utterly ignored made her feel outcast, brushed aside as a burdensome parasite, causing too much hassle for both tribes to waste time and energy on.

Did she belong anywhere at all? Not really, with the exception of possibly her father if she took Charlie out of the equation.

After the sixth and final chemotherapy, she had felt at her worst, practically lame and still needing to embark on the tedious return journey. The nurse had offered to arrange a wheelchair for her to be brought to the Maggie's Centre to recuperate prior to travelling back. There they would make her a cup of tea, have a chat and a volunteer might drive her all the way home.

She had agreed for the simple reason that there seemed no better option. Wheeled about by a total and non-communicative stranger, to whom she had to do her utmost to show gratitude for doing her a favour, she'd felt like a real dependent invalid. That day had been the day that walking unaided had also come to an end. Filled to overflowing with despair, she had been deposited only a couple of metres over the doorstep and left there, delegated to the next department, a phenomenon she had become familiar with. She had grown used to waiting endless waits and react with stoic silence. Hence, she had sat, had stared directly in front of her and had gone blank.

A blank mind had occurred more and more often. The brain still functioned and functioned well, but it took breaks frequently. Was also that seemingly final active part of her going on the blink, then she had even more to worry about, but it took a mind, a brain to worry. Maybe it was a good thing after all then that her brain became dysfunctional, for it would stop endless worrying. What a relief it was going to be to gain thoughtless spaciousness after all those weeks and months of ongoing worries. On the other hand, loosing her marbles as well as bodily functions might well be the final straw.

"Why were you left here in the middle of the entrance hall all by yourself, I wonder?"

The female voice pulled her out of a non-existent reverie. Resolutely the handles were grabbed and with a jolt of her head a next person started her moving, first turning around, then forward.

"Come on in."

Uninvited Guest, Unexpected Gifts

Her brain began functioning once again. She noticed what a silly remark it was, inviting her to come on in, whilst her movements were from now on being limited to other people's goodness of heart towards her, the dependant. All she herself could muster was thinking about moving or wishing to move somewhere. To translate a thought or wish into an actual action, her brain and limbs would need rewiring. Who would do that for her and how long might that take? She saw no light at the end of the tunnel yet and that alone deepened despair.

What deepened despair further still, was the suspicion, that also this woman would be a cancer survivor. All volunteers had had cancer of some sort, apparently and all patients she'd met, ditto. Conversing with people without cancer in past or present had faded into a grey and distant past, like Dominique and the others from the bank. Could she still call them colleagues? People like Gwyneth and the other choir members. Would they accept her back if she survived and regained some level of physical capacity? Was she ever going to fit back into some kind of normal life or was this it, a new normality to have to get used to?

From way far came the question, if she'd like a cup of tea.

She nodded and wondered whether her fingers still harboured enough resilience to lift a full cup all the way to her mouth without spilling. The first time she'd been here, she'd spilled coffee all over her trousers and the sofa. If she spilled again, that was her reputation fixed as the woman in the wheelchair who always spills and staff would refuse to be on duty, when she was likely to appear.

But then again, today had been the last chemotherapy and she wouldn't return in such a sorry state. Maybe.

Tension rigidified her fingers, hands and arms when she was handed the coffee. In full concentration she took a sip. It was boiling and burned her lips, but she persisted and kept sipping. Better her lips burned than spilling any and creating another negative reputation for herself. The taste was insignificant in comparison and when the woman asked, whether she was enjoying it, she nodded once more and tried not to loose the momentum. Afterwards, her lips felt sensitive, but she'd caused no spillage.

"You certainly enjoyed that." said the woman and took the mug out of her hand.

"Yes, I did, thank you."

Several people were sitting or wandering about. Some were busy and others were in conversation. Some were sitting on their own and some wore a headscarf like herself. Some were bold and had no qualms about showing it and some had hair growing back as a thin downy layer. Was hers going to regrow similarly? If it all?

"Are you also going through chemotherapy?"

The cynical part of her wanted to scream: "Stupid question, silly cow. Isn't it obvious that I belong to this doomed category? Why else do you think I turn up on your doorstep in a wheelchair with a headscarf as badge, as sign of belonging to your club? Do you really expect that I come here out of hobby?"

The civilised part of her answered: "Yes. Actually, no. Not any more. Just now was the final dose."

"Good on you. What did you have?"

"You mean, how often within what kind of time frame? Six with three weeks in between."

"O, that one. That's more or less standard procedure for women with breast cancer? Is that what you have? Or had, hopefully?"

"Had, yes. About four months ago they took all malignant tissue out and the chemo seemed nothing more than precaution to reduce the chance of secondary cancer."

"Indeed. Standard procedures. Great that it's all over now for you. Recovery starts today. Try not to loose patience, because it will be slow, but pretty soon you'll notice some sense of normality to return in your energy levels and that you're capable of just doing just that tiny bit more. Try to take encouragement out of these teenchyweenchy baby steps. They mean a lot in the beginning. How have these last months been?"

"In the beginning it was fine and I thought all these warnings of severe side effect to be pure exaggeration. After the third one, hell broke loose. The worst day of my life it was. Yes, you could call it that. By far. After that followed nine weeks of ongoing and relentless incapacitated hell."

"Yeah, pretty rough, huh?"

"I'm tired, incredibly tired."

"Would you like me to let you be for a while and check up on you a bit later?"

"If you don't mind? You're ever so kind."

"Not at all, that's what we're here for."

"I haven't even asked you about your situation. Sorry."

"Not to worry. If you wish, I'll tell you later. For now rest seems your best bet. Shall I get you some cushions?"

The woman did and made sure she was comfortable. In no time she dozed and on waking she had no idea how long she had slept or where she was. Her mouth had been dribbling, though, as if she were senile and in her eighties. When would incontinence commence? Once her initial concerns wore off, it felt liberating to not wake up in the imprisonment of home.

Quite a few people occupied themselves with whatever kind of busy-ness within a quiet and relaxed atmosphere. Nobody seemed to have a care in the world.

She sighed in a relaxed kind of way. Next to her stood a table with quite a collection of magazines and books, each of them related to cancer, naturally. A thin publication caught her eye: "Cancer, a healer's perspective – Insights, stories and messages of hope." Hope was what she needed most of all. She reached out her hand to take a closer look. Before the hand, forced to move in slow motion, reached the brain's target, she was being interrupted.

"You've woken up. Well, you surely are a sound sleeper. Do you feel any better?"

She dropped back into the wheelchair and answered

positively.

Uninvited Guest, Unexpected Gifts

CHAPTER FIFTEEN

The woman at Maggie's Centre had been right: the ongoing
and relentless incapacitated hell eased. Way too slow for her
liking, but she'd also been warned against impatience and to
not overdo things as soon as she would feel the slightest bit of
energy returning.

Funnily enough, the first indication had been one morning
when brushing her teeth. Such an uncomplicated routine she
had performed from when she was knee high to a grasshopper.
For months the familiar routine had been close to a gamble,
aiming to squeeze the paste onto the brush. Control over the
simplest of gestures had been lacking and paste had often
spilled over sink and floor, which gave her even more to clean
up and waste her energy on and where to find that extra
energy? Gosh, life had made her feel stupid at times.

The routine job had flowed with ease on this particular
morning, an easy flow she had become unaccustomed to. The

success didn't register at first, but once it dawned, she had brushed her teeth thrice, because all good things come in threes. After that, brushing her teeth became a habit, forever linked with celebration.

The six hospital trips had been by far the most demanding. Unimaginable the amount of energy, effort and concentration those commuting trips had taken and imagine that only a few months ago, she'd walked distances, descended and ascended in and out of underground stations and boarded one tube after the other without giving it a second thought. And suddenly, she had dreaded arriving at a station where she needed to change or when she'd reached her final destination and needed to stumble as far as her front door.

In public she so much wanted to appear normal in order to be included in the daily goings on once more, albeit only for a few hours. The very fact that the weather was warm and she wore head scarves was a clear give away. If only she'd been Muslim or the queen, she would get away with it. Now the headgear branded her, how she imagined Anne Frank, wearing a David star during the second world war, had been branded, doomed to suffer hardship prior to an untimely, cruel death.

Those horrors faded into the past. The teeth brushing victory contributed to deleting months of doom and gloom from her memory, although, not instantly. Of course not. She kept reminding herself that she was only in the earliest of beginning stages of regaining a tiny bit of vitality. Patience was of the utmost importance and in that she forced obedience upon herself, deeply frustrating as it was.

She wanted to act, to do, to venture out, to go shopping, to wander through the park, to take the train to Richmond, to sit on a terrace, to go to a pub, to eat out in her favourite Greek restaurant. She wanted. She wanted. She wanted. For the simple reason, that she felt capable and hadn't had any capacity for ever to move beyond medical dates.

To prove a point last week, she had grabbed a bottle of water, flung the handbag over a now pain free left shoulder and had locked the door behind her.

It had been three days after she'd had an MRI scan and that had been three weeks after her last treatment. Maybe it was imagination, maybe wishful thinking, but that last hospital trip had taken less out of her, it felt. The rest of the day and the next, the previously drained sense of utter exhaustion hadn't materialised like before. Did that signal another victory or another cause for celebration?

To prove a point last week, after she'd locked the door behind her, she had intended to celebrate by treating herself to a cappuccino in the café around the corner, or if wind and warmth allowed, on their terrace in the pedestrianised area.

The words of warning of the Maggie's woman had still lingered fresh in her memory and she promised not to overdo things and try to resist temptations.

Once she had locked the door behind her for a first outing not involving medical procedures, elation had overcome her and a sudden rush of adrenaline had caused a slight dizziness. Only for ten seconds or so she'd required support from the banister. Once the attack had subsided, she'd reached the street, her street without further mishaps. Warned and encouraged in succession, she'd found the terrace in balmy sunshine and reasonably sheltered from the breeze.

She'd chosen a seat, carefully, facing the sun. Facing the sun. Facing the sunshine warming her facial skin. The gentle rays had felt like the sweetest caress she had ever received. It had made her cry soft tears of a deeply moving gratitude for the simplest of pleasures. How she had missed such pleasures. How had she managed to survive without? She was pretty resilient after all.

And when the waiter had brought cappuccino, he'd completed a heavenly indulgence for his customer, unbeknown to himself. The generous tip had taken him by surprise, though. For him it had been a first that somebody paid for a single coffee with a tenner and wanted no change.

She had sat and sipped and breathed and watched the world

go by and not pass her by any longer. That horrendous phase she was leaving behind now. Here and now, life became worth living, symbolised by a medium cappuccino. Millions of people all over the world would order and enjoy a similar drink today and not give it any thought at all. Such luxuries were so easily taken for granted. Also she had taken such pleasures for granted and had grossly undervalued the immensity and intensity of tiny pleasures. From now on, also after having regained perfect health, she was going to take no simple enjoyment for granted ever again, but unreservedly absorb the joy.

Back in the flat, she had been totally chuffed, had run a hot bath, had switched on some relaxing music on repeat, had gone to bed and had slept a solid two hours of restful sleep.

She'd woken up feeling replenished and upbeat, for the first time in months actually looking forward to something, even, belief it or not, looking forward to visiting hospital that following day for a consultation with the oncologist to receive her scan results.

Uninvited Guest, Unexpected Gifts

CHAPTER SIXTEEN

The meeting with the oncologist lasted longer than foreseen,
due to certain complications and questions her situation raised,
as well as the lengthy discussions about which course of
action to take.

On exiting the consultation room, she felt, for a second time,
devastated and caught in a maze of options and choices.
Choices expected to be made by herself once she'd had the
opportunity to let the radically changed situation and the
consequent options sink in and digest.

After leaving the consultation room, the maze of troubled
ponderings made her unaware of the direction her legs
wandered. Awareness dawned, after a voice asked whether
she'd prefer a tea or a coffee. On automatic pilot she had
headed to the only location on the huge compound, The
Maggie's Centre, where she might find whatever solace, a
willingly listening ear and perhaps discuss the latest

developments with some experienced people.

Before answering, she reflected briefly on the fact that somebody else had pushed her as far as the entrance hall in a wheelchair a few weeks earlier. This time she had walked, unaided. The quite significant progress hadn't even registered and why should it? What was the use of dwelling on skimpy improvements, when, in comparison, today's tidings of disaster well and truly overshadowed all progress, however significant on its own merit.

"Coffee, please, thank you."

The answer came across like an order, rather than a response to a favour. She was well aware of the mishap, but energy and motivation to correct her tone of voice were lacking. Instead, she remembered the very first visit to Maggie's and how deeply she had sunk into that sofa. In her present state of mind sofa was synonymous to hiding, to becoming invisible to the outside world. Yes, it had made her spill coffee but that had been due to her lame arm as well as the unexpected extreme softness. Today she would be better prepared. Besides that, she hadn't spilled any coffee the second time round and in the meantime her arm had healed. For now at least. For how long, though?

She sank into cushions and sofa. Encapsulation in soft material provided comfort of some sort, as did the coffee on arrival, as did the woman who brought it.

"You don't look like a happy bunny, if you don't mind me saying so. Do you care for a chat? By the way, my name is Brenda. And yours?"

"Don't bother about my name. As soon as you'll memorise it, it will have grown into a useless piece of information, Brenda. Thank you for coming to sit with me. I can do with a chat."

"Sounds like it. I'm here for you. Do you want to tell me what's the matter?"

"I've just received the worst possible news from the oncologist. My death sentence more or less. Although, obviously, he used different terminology. Last year I was

116

diagnosed with breast cancer. Over the last several months I have been operated on and had six chemo treatments. After the operation, the news was positive. He said, they had removed all malignant tissues and had even removed all lymph nodes on the affected side, as a precautionary measure. Not that he had asked for my consent beforehand. But OK, that's by the by. I can live with that. If I will live, that is. In order to prevent cancer cells being activated again, he recommended chemo to kill them off. That's customary recommendation and generally accepted as the most effective method to avoid secondary cancer. And I went along with the advice. Naturally so. How do I know what's best for me? They're the experts and routinely deal with similar cases day after day, week in week out. In a nutshell, the chemo dragged me to hell and back, pulled me through a hedge backwards, did all the usual things and had all the regular side effects. You'll be familiar with it all, no doubt?"

"I am. We hear your kind of story on a daily basis and I've been through it all myself, believe you me."

"Thought as much. Don't you get fed up and drained, listening to the same old, dreadfully boring and depressing story a million times? Doesn't it make you sick hearing it?"

"No. I know it serves a function. It helps and supports people who are often at their wits end. Besides that, not all stories are bad news, fortunately. And together we have a great team. That's a damn good support system for ourselves. Therefore, don't you worry about us. We're here for you. What was the news you received this morning? Not what you expected to hear, apparently."

"Absolutely not. In such an insensitive, matter-of-fact kind of way I'm being told that a certain conglomeration of malignant cellular material had remained active in the breast, close to the nipple. According to him, that area in particular is highly sensitive with high concentrations of nerve endings. Increased sensitivity increases the risk of the reactivation of cancer. He made it sound plausible, theoretically. At the same

117

time, his tone of voice made it sound as if he wasn't sure himself either or as if he was deliberately hiding some crucial piece of information. Of course, I didn't question him, taken aback as I was."

Brenda prevented the ensuing silence from lasting for any awkward length of time: "Understandably so. What are they planning for you?"

"They are not planning anything. He presented me with a series of options and advised me to think it over and come to a decision as soon as possible, inform him and he'd honour my wish. That is how he put it. Honour my wish. My wish is for that first operation to have been an unparalleled success, so I wouldn't have to face another onslaught. You'll probably know just as well as I do, that survival rates of patients with secondary cancer are negligible. Today I've been dumped into that virtually hopeless category."

"What did he give as options?"

"Stronger chemo more frequently, mastectomy, radio therapy. The holy trinity of advanced breast cancer. What a prospect, hey Brenda? Cheers to that."

"The standard procedures. Do you already have an inkling what your choice will be? It wouldn't surprise me a single bit, if you haven't got the foggiest yet."

"Indeed I haven't. Why bother in the first place? Why bother torturing my body further if there is a nigh on certain death sentence hanging over me? Why not refuse all medical procedures and say "What the heck" and live, travel, tick all the boxes of my bucket list. Not that I have one. Why would I expect to be in need of a bucket list at this stage of my life? But, I can easily come up with a long list. Too long for my remaining short life. Short it will be. Listen to me. I'm only thirty five and I'm contemplating dying. How revolting. How depressing is that?"

"Do you really think it will be that bad?"

"Don't tell me that you perceive any of these options, or a possible combination thereof, to be a laughing matter. Chemo wrecked me these last months. I'm bald. I've often been sick. I've hardly eaten for months, lost loads of weight and body mass and feel tired, tired, tired. You can't imagine, how utterly exhausted and kaputt I've been feeling and still feel. Now they even want me to undergo stronger, more frequent chemo before or after loosing a breast or both. Both before or after the operation, I mean. Not necessarily both breasts to be removed. Well, why not actually? They might as well. Out of precaution with my best interest at heart, naturally. Like they removed all lymph nodes without my permission. Sorry for sounding so cynical, Brenda."

"It's OK. Express what you feel right now. It's absolutely fine with me. Does part of you see any positivity or any hope at all?"

"Don't know. Not now, that's for sure. Do you see any hope for me?"

"Difficult for me to say. As long as there is life, there is also hope. I truly believe in that after everything I have been through myself, but if you ask me what the best route will be for you to take, I can't possibly give any kind of recommendation. In that we are not medical experts and hence limited in providing advice and give any kind of prognosis or state any preference. Whichever steps you decide to take, however, we'll support you to the very best of our ability."

"But, hope you can not give me?"

"Not in the way you feel you need right now. But most likely our moral, mental or emotional support can rekindle a bit of hope. There will always be somebody here for you, promise. From eight till eight. Seven days a week. Not always the same people, of course. Even over here we work in shifts."

"That alone is reassuring. Thank you."

The women sat in silence for a while. The one woman waited quietly to see whether any other assistance was needed. The other woman looked directly ahead of her to the floor or let her eyes wander.

The wandering eyes rested on the reading table with that

collection of magazines and other cancer related publications. Vaguely her well functioning brain remembered one little book, she'd been about to pick up last time. The cover had been blueish grey, depicting a seascape. She didn't see it lying about any longer. The name of the author and the title had slipped from memory, but one word of the subtitle had stuck in her mind: "hope".

Hope.

"Please give me a fair dose of that", she thought. "Because the way things are turning out, I've none. None whatsoever."

All these Maggie's women had survived. That in itself was hopeful. But then again, had there been any cases of secondary cancer among them? Unlikely, she thought and didn't dare ask, in case her suspicion would be confirmed.

It had become crystal clear to her, that women like Brenda were nice, way more than just nice. They showed a self-sacrificing generosity and then not the self-sacrifice her mum had fallen victim to, bending over backwards to please others, mainly her husband, her father. The women here did not act out of a marital obligation, but for them it was a conscious choice to serve, like a calling, like embarking on a mission. Their sacrifice served a wider purpose for people like herself, who landed in a hopeless position. To be of service in such a way had to be fulfilling. Although, providing hope where there was none in the first place, they were not capable of either. Magicians waving a magic wand existed only in fairy tales and life was no fairy tale, most definitely not.

She closed her eyes and tried to recall the cover of the book with the exact wording. Photographic memory, normally a strong point, failed her and she asked Brenda.

Brenda remembered seeing it, but according to her, books displayed the curious habit of continually appearing out of nowhere and disappearing again and no, also she didn't remember the title or the name of the author. A subtitle she had not noticed, but if it might be of help, she would ask the team to check if anybody else had an idea and let her know once she

Uninvited Guest, Unexpected Gifts

had discovered more details.

CHAPTER SEVENTEEN

She googled "hope".

All the way back from the hospital her mind had known only one focal point: hope. Now that she belonged in the category of secondary cancer patients, virtually synonymous to terminally ill cancer patients, the chance of survival had reduced to ..... To what? To twenty percent? To ten percent? More? Less?

She could have asked the oncologist, but how to think rationally when the world had been collapsing all around her? His tone of voice and his slight hesitation kept bothering her. Was that what he had been trying to hide? Purely the fact that she was suddenly classed as a terminally ill case with an extremely low percentage chance of recovery and the complementary percentage indicating her death sentence? There was no point in guessing which of the two numbers was the highest and which the lowest. The notion made her shiver.

Uninvited Guest, Unexpected Gifts

Had the surgeon blundered? Had he not been accurate enough and overlooked affected tissues? Had he been in too much of a hurry for whatever reason to pay proper attention? Had he categorised her case as a run of the mill standard procedure and therefore approached the surgery with a certain element of carelessness? She had no idea and she would probably never know the full truth.

In the darkest regions of her stomach, rage was shimmering. It made her queasy and she had to burp, but didn't want to. Burping felt risqué as if the release of trapped air would burst a dam and then what? What if a dam burst she wasn't even aware she had internalised? What might that dam contain and hold back? What kind of force, unbeknown to herself, had she stored behind lock and key? She didn't want to go there. She didn't dare enter the arena of her internal battle ground and what good would it do anyway? It was only going to make misery drill deeper still into her psyche and she really didn't need any more of that. No, she needed the opposite. She needed hope.

Hope.

That's why, all the way back from hospital she focused on that four letter word and the focus continued once she had arrived home. Without giving her mind a single second of rest, the word kept swirling around in her thoughts relentlessly. So much so, that, when she stuck the key in the keyhole and rotated the door handle, it occurred to her, that she had no idea how she had arrived. The streets, the stations, the tubes, the people, the shops and window displays, nothing had registered. She had travelled in the haze of a preoccupied mind with no other focus than hope, hope and nothing but hope.

How to take the notion of hope further? She didn't know what possessed her, because a very alien drive took hold of her, a weird knowing that she had to get hold of that book. A strange sense occupied every segment of her physique and of her racing thoughts, that therein, in that book, may well lie her rescue, her one and only source of hope.

But how, how to find the correct details, when all she recalled was one word of the subtitle and nothing else. A bookshop could make head nor tail out of such limited information and amazon was clever, but not that clever. She herself had to do the research and in theatrical, dramatic language, she envisaged herself on a vision quest for her holy grail of hope. That was to become her undertaking. Search for the holy grail of hope, her hope and nobody else's.

She googled hope for hours on end. Hope combined with stories. Hope combined with reports. Hope combined with messages. Hope combined with tales. Hope combined with experiences. Hope combined with insights. Hope combined with one, two or three of the nouns mentioned above and many other synonyms. She thanked the people who had invented a computer accessible thesaurus.

Whilst obsessed with her holy crusade for hope, she didn't bother about wearing her headscarf. Normally she did in case the doorbell rang and she had to be presentable to the outside world. Not covering her skull and wandering around bald headed, felt confrontationally liberating somehow.

And a wig had felt much weirder still. She'd been to fit one, however, none had had her own colouring, none had had a similar softness, none had had the shine. Instead, each had felt artificially plasticized and tight. As tight as tights or as tight as she imagined a condom would feel around a man's penis. She'd known beforehand it wouldn't be her thing. Charlie had insisted on her having one fitted and had even offered to come along, in all likelihood to have a giggle, secretly or openly, at her expense. And why had that woman insisted? So as not to be confronted by the naked truth and by human, i.e. her own, mortality? Had that been the underlying reason she'd attempted to get her stepdaughter to cover up reality?

The shop assistant had been ever so understanding, kind and compassionate and had learned all the correct and polite phrases by heart, but had made no sale.

There she sat, bald headed, like a raving lunatic, or like a silently determined woman on a mission or, basically, each in turn. She searched, she focused, she typed, she concentrated, she scrolled, she racked her brain.

The brain functioned well, but returning the cover in question back to memory in enough detail to decipher the writing was too much to ask apparently, frustrating as it was.

"Patience. Patience", reminded her mind.

"True", answered her impatient self, "but I've practised patience for eternity. My life depends on hope and nothing else. That's the only goal I'll pursue from now on and nothing else, because hope is what I'm in need of. Now."

619.000.000 in 0.28 seconds – 203.000.000 in 0.30 seconds – 50.200.000 in 0.50 seconds – 173.000.000 in 0.30 seconds and so it went on. Word after word followed combination after combination followed hour after hour followed day after day. In the end she lost count of how many days she had sat at her desk, bent over screen and keyboard and oblivious to all else within a feverish bubble. A successful or unsuccessful search turned into a matter of life or death in the most literal sense of the words.

When she googled the combination "Insights and messages of hope", she finally hit the jackpot. Eureka. She screamed a euphoric scream for the whole neighbourhood to hear and applauded herself and her stubbornness and jumped up and down in her seat and drummed the desk, unable to contain her elation. That determined stubbornness paid off.

The screen showed the book's full title, subtitle, author's name and a photograph of the cover: "Cancer, a healer's perspective - Insights, messages and stories of hope." Indeed, the recognition of the blueish grey hazy photograph of the seascape was instant. The book was readily available via Amazon.

Once she had ordered it, without further ado or procrastination, she couldn't wait for it to arrive and suffered two sleepless nights as a result. Two sleepless nights focused on a feverish hope.

CHAPTER EIGHTEEN

It didn't take long to read the eighty pages, because, in the end, eighty pages are only eighty pages. That was not the only reason, though. The "Insights, stories and messages of hope" instilled positivity into her and she devoured them and lapped up what had lacked for months. Incapable of reaching saturation point, she didn't tire any longer.

Amazingly enough, one of the two real life stories, described a woman about two decades older than herself, but facing a strikingly similar situation in that her mother had also died of cancer when in her teens. She had nursed her night and day until the terminal breath had finally given relief. Also this daughter had swallowed grief, sorrow, anger and had been scared of copying her mother, of dying way too young due to following in mother's footsteps.

The book turned out to be an incredible eye opener, so unexpectedly inspiring, that she was unable to avert her eyes.

Uninvited Guest, Unexpected Gifts

Flabbergasted by the coincidence of reading about her own predicament from a total stranger's perspective, made her skin crawl and tears surface. No wonder she had felt a feverish urge to track down the publication and get her hands on it as soon as possible. The intuitive flash at the Maggie's proved its worth and she was mighty chuffed she hadn't ignored it.

The story didn't reveal, whether the woman's cancer had been primary or secondary. Even if it turned out to be "only" primary, she had survived the illness and had healed resulting in a clear scan.

Would secondary cancer really make that much of a difference?

This woman's hope had also been thin on the ground, actually way, way thinner, because she'd had only three more months left to live, according to the medical profession. Three months only. Imagine how unimaginably frightened will she have been. She couldn't picture herself facing such a stark diagnosis. Her own oncologist had not provided a time scale and she was most definitely not as close to death's door as her predecessor had been. And that stranger had survived. Despite having only three months of life left, scan results had been all clear. Indeed all clear, after what read like a quite spooky and creepy series of treatments, bordering on exorcism on occasion.

Over and over again she read and reread the story, as if she wanted to learn it by heart, to imprint the message into her brain cells for once and for all, to never ever forget the possibility, the possibility of hope, the possibility of healing.

Hope indeed. Here it was, the hopeful message she had longed for with all her heart and soul. Here, in print, black on white and that was precisely why she had invested so much time and energy googling her vague recollection of the title and ordering the publication.

Was her oncologist going to be supportive of her taking this, so-called alternative route? The one in the story hadn't been. He hadn't been unsupportive and hadn't judged his patient either, but he'd been professionally unable to give an opinion about non-scientific approaches. Maybe it would be best not to rub her oncologist up the wrong way and keep it quiet.

Keep what quiet? Out of the blue it dawned how her mind wandered, for she found herself speaking, or rather thinking, as if she'd already made up her mind to go and consult this guy, the author. What a funny idea and scary in a way, because, what would she let herself into? What would she be exposed to? Would he be genuine or a crook, a charlatan after her pennies like that Californian dream analysis institute had treated, or, rather, mistreated her and had abused her vulnerability and desperate predicament without delivering anything of value after cashing her pennies.

If she did decide to bite the bullet, was she ready, though, to undergo exorcism? Was she prepared to risk spells of insanity, for that was very much what it sounded like. Would she allow such extreme vulnerability and would she be forced to sob, wail and curse in a similar fashion and if she refused to or couldn't, would she blow her ultimate chance of survival? Question after question kept surfacing.

OK, the woman involved had had cancer of the liver, not breast cancer, but would that be very different, though? Would the one be easier or harder to cure than the other and why did the tumour appear in the liver with the one person and in the breast with the other? Which circumstances determined the location of a tumour? Was there a reasoning behind it or did the body have its own mind, so to speak and chose at random where to plant a tumour, just for the fun of it or because that was the way the penny dropped or the dice rolled for the person in question.

The more often she read that particular chapter, the more questions arose, which was pretty annoying really. She decided to write them all down, for each and every one of those questions seemed too precious to forget. Each seemed to hold a different key to her life.

A list of twenty five questions was the result and after

writing down the last one, she felt complete, simultaneously also depleted. Reading the book after days of laden anticipation and having thousands of thoughts running through her mind as a result and to top it all, questioning the theories, projected onto her own present state of being according to the oncologist's prognosis, felt all in all like a huge undertaking. Not just that, today's revelations turned her way of thinking about her and cancer and her prospects upside down, back to front or inside out, from a certain death sentence to still a fair chance of recovery, resulting in a life worth living.

It was the brightest and at the same time the toughest day's work for months. She treated herself to a well deserved long soak in the bath, prepared and ate a hearty meal with real appetite and slept a sound sleep.

CHAPTER NINETEEN

The plane landed in an airport with one international flight daily and one arrival hall only, whilst passengers exited directly onto the road. Surprised curiosity made her ask about the actual number of departure gates. One, came the reply and for some peculiar reason the almost primitive welcome fitted her adventure, embarking on something totally new. An excited apprehension had knotted her stomach for days now. As soon as she stood outside, she took a deep breath.

The air tasted crispy, clear and pure.

The car stood ready and waiting for her at the rental office. That facility was at least available and she'd been recommended to rent a car at the airport.

Apparently, there was a regular bus service, but those timetables gave less freedom of movement and she might also like to do some sightseeing during her time off. The guy had made it sound as if she was planning to enrol in a college of some sort.

The car rental assistant put her suitcase in the boot and took all the time in the world to give directions in great detail.

Off she went, on quiet roads, which included the main A road. Why did she catch herself often breathing incredibly deep? Why did copious tears flow suddenly? The road, virtually traffic free as it was, became a blur and she needed and found a parking place.

Standing still, she checked her new surroundings with only a few scattered houses and farms, without a town or village in sight anywhere. On the right side hills rolled, rounded and gently, gradually rising towards an open horizon with scattered woodlands and farmers' fields. On the left side, an open stretch of water ended in impressive cliffs in front of mountains, where smidgens of snow still hadn't melted. Space, was all she could think of and so unbelievably much of it. Quiet, was yet another word that sprang to mind. The few cars zooming by barely disturbed the quietude, not even the occasional lorry, even though those shook her car. They belonged somehow.

Strange. Tears flowed again when that particular thought passed by.

Belonged. To belong. Belonging.

"A funny habit." she thought, "how I keep tasting words."

Tasting words only seemed to occur when a word gained in importance in that moment, under these specific circumstances. Like "rise", when she'd been physically unable to. Yucky, how scary had that morning been and she shivered at the memory. Like "hope", when that had remained the sole life's quality left to her, apparently, in her then desolate state. That same hope had transported her here, to this parking place in the middle of nowhere. The surroundings were beautiful, without a shadow of a doubt, but they did not ooze hope yet.

Belonging.

How did that fit? She couldn't imagine herself belonging in these regions. Beautiful and quiet it boasted pure air, but the sense of isolation might well creep upon her. Patience, she urged herself, patience, wait and see how "belonging" was going to fit into the greater scheme of things.

She drove on, traced the town in question and the B&B easily enough and settled in. The smooth flow added up to a pleasant and convenient start.

Her first appointment was scheduled early next morning, two miles out of town at the healer's home. In order to arrive well prepared and give it her best shot, she went to bed early. Sleep didn't come easily though, for thoughts ruled for well over half of the night, but they were not worrying thoughts specifically. They were more just random thought patterns running riot, disturbing a good night's sleep, but nothing of the heavy kind and definitely not the kind of heavy thinking she had grown used to. If somebody would have asked her the following morning, what she had been thinking of, she couldn't have said.

In the morning, one fragment of a dream returned to her conscious memory. Again she'd observed a serene, wooded scene and again with abundant bird song. Yet again, astonishingly enough, there'd been a unicorn in all its shiny and translucent splendour. This time she hadn't been kneeling, but had stood next to it, bathing in the animal's shininess and revelling in its radiance. Her fingers had stroked the mane. Fingertips touched and didn't touch, because the fingertips felt and didn't feel. The fingertips sensed and didn't sense. She'd been left with the memory of a most peculiar feeling. The silken softness had been transparent to the touch, there was no more accurate way to describe the unearthliness of the overall sensation.

No further details of the dream were surfacing, even though she tried hard to remember more. What remained, was some strange prickling in her fingertips, as if they'd become highly sensitised overnight. It made her relive the multitude of sensations her body had lived through in a time span of about ten months from the moment her fingertips had first discovered this lump.

The initial indication of a spontaneous growth had been less than a year ago and the lump had refused to be ignored. It had grown all by itself without her having any control over it. Procrastination had prevented her from having it checked, like that funny game had predicted. After that, the actual diagnosis had been a bitter pill to swallow. The operation and the post-operative period hadn't been a big deal, but the six doses of chemotherapy had taken its toll on body as well as mind and she wouldn't wish that on anyone. If recovery from the preceding medical procedures had been the concluding stage, she'd long be back at work by now. The sledgehammer of the second bout of bad news about her secondary cancer, had knocked her for six or could have done. Actually it had, come to think of it, woken her up into taking charge. How she had arrived at the Maggie's in a totally blurred haze that day, utterly unawares, she would never forget. What had guided her then and what had made her want to pick up that little book on the previous visit and had brought it back to memory?

A mysterious step by step unfolding had led to her sleeping in this strange bed in this unfamiliar town in order to meet the author of that little book, a so-called healer.

Next morning, armoured with directions and the list of twenty five questions, she went on her way. She left a bit early, because she didn't want him to have to wait, for, doubtlessly, he'd be in huge demand. Four weeks she had had to wait before he was able to fit her into his diary. Not that long, actually, although, each extra day added insecurity, tension and increased her anxiety. Each extra day might result in cancer spreading further and a cure becoming less of a possibility.

Signposts were lacking, therefore it became a slight gamble to determine, which driveway was the correct one. There was not a row of cars parked outside and it was nothing like what she expected the premises of a private cancer clinic to look like. But then, what did she anticipate? Haloes? Banners with

Christ images? Placards welcoming patients to the palace of healing? None of the above applied when she simply drove towards a normal house amidst normal flowering gardens surrounded by normal agricultural fields and woods.

The man, she recognised him from the picture on the back cover of the book was dressed in a white t-shirt and black trousers and walked in flip-flops. He exited the house as if he'd been waiting for her arrival and once she'd closed the car door behind her, he stretched out his hand, shook hers and said:

"You made it, Esther. Welcome. Was your trip OK and is the B&B looking after you well?"

Accompanied by his relaxed banter, she was invited inside, guided to the treatment room and asked to take a seat.

Suddenly it dawned on her that he mentioned her name. For months now it had only been her father and Charlie, who had called her by her Christian name during their habitual Sunday visits. Her colleagues and choir members had done as well, naturally, but they hadn't been in touch during all these months of illness and all medical staff had consistently called her Ms. Crompton.

Even though it had been her name for over three decades, it almost took getting used to being called it again, especially by a stranger. But then, what had she expected? More formality and to be addressed by her surname or to be addressed as Ms. with or without surname? To be called Esther throughout the week ahead felt right.

On entering the treatment room, she spotted a blueish purple box on a chest of drawers. Surprise took over and before she managed to stop herself, she asked, whether he also played that Transformation Game. When he explained he was a trained facilitator and inquired how come she was familiar with the game, she burst into a monologue.

She spoke about the game she had played just before getting ill and about the card "procrastination" and about the angel of "Trust" and the depicted unicorn. Then she spoke about that

134

first dream in great detail and she also described the dream from the previous night and the strange tingling sensations her fingers had been left with.

He interrupted a few times, like when she told him that the unicorn's hoof had circled her right breast three times. He asked in which direction the circling motion had went and when her hand indicated the circle, he nodded and said "Great. Clockwise, a positive sign."

She was too preoccupied to notice and talked non-stop for well over fifteen minutes and concluded with an apology for wasting so much precious time.

He smiled and urged her not to apologise. Her stories were most definitely not a waste of time. Listening to her and observing her body language as well as the energetic fluctuations in her aura and in certain energy points, called chakras, provided him with essential information, he explained, which, in the long run, made it easier to work effectively with her.

And when she asked, overcome with shyness, what kind of information she had given away without realising, he replied matter-of-factly that she was a bit nervous, understandably so, that she needed to get a lot off her chest, that the little girl Esther, who believed fervently in the world of myths and fairy tales, had been enthralled by the magic of the dream and that this realm didn't receive the acknowledgement it deserved from the adult woman and that she therefore denied part of her true self. Her heart chakra and her soul seat had brightened whilst she'd recounted the dream. Observing her, made him wonder, whether she often denied such essential aspects of her true self and which other aspects had been denied over the years. He left the question unanswered, but instead stated that they would unravel such and similar issues to get an idea of the underlying emotional and mental factors possibly contributing to her attracting cancer. The sensitivity in her fingers after waking up, he put down to the energy already beginning to flow, partly freed up by the dream, by a trust aspect awakening and in an unconscious preparation for their work to commence this morning. A large part of the therapy happened outside of treatments via energetic transmission, he explained.

He sounded enthusiastic when explaining about her fingers and in reply to the question, whether he made sense, she merely nodded, too much taken aback by the amount of information she'd given away through her babble.

Would she like to get more off her chest?

Oh yes. Tons. However, if he gave her free reign, there'd be no opportunity for her to do the real work, she objected.

What if this was the real work, he suggested and what if her unburdening was part and parcel of her healing process? Frequently, he explained, a first session was predominantly verbal, giving a clear indication of what to focus on in later sessions. Besides that, it established a sense of trust and without a trusting relationship no healing was possible.

Without aiming to convince her, he spoke in a relaxed way. His relaxation eased Esther's anxiety. She couldn't help but notice how tightness, in her shoulders for example, eased somewhat and how she inhaled deeply, once, involuntarily, as if letting go of tension and nervousness.

Did he notice her deep breath and subsequent sigh? Most likely, because he appeared to notice everything and that felt scary. She felt as transparent as the unicorn had been in her dream, vulnerable and exposed to the core. Is that what she came here for? The woman in his book had exposed herself well and truly and she had been healed despite a medical prognosis of only three months to live. "Hope. Trust. Unicorn." she reminded herself.

In response to his prompting to relate her cancer story from its earliest beginning to the present, a second outpouring started.

He listened, wrote a few things down, made the occasional remark and asked further details at times.

Another fifteen minutes or so passed without actual healing

work, she noticed at the end of her second monologue and when she told him, almost reprimanded him, his smile reappeared and he said, that she no longer seemed to be setback by procrastination. She dropped into a silent pondering for a moment. Until the question blurted forth, literally out of nowhere, whether he could heal her.

"Well, Esther, we'll see what we can do. I can't promise. I'll do my best, like I always do and results are at times great, but not always. The fact is, that you have a done a fair bit of preparative inner work yourself....."

"Did I?" she thought. "How? What does he mean?"

"..... which gives us a head start. You seem to trust it here ....."

"Do I? ..... Yes, I do", she thought.

".... and that in itself is vitally important. Would you like to lie down?"

"Yes, please."

What followed was a brief explanation of what she could expect. He encouraged her to close her eyes and not to try and follow his actions or analyse them. The more she managed to allow her mind to quieten down and her body to do its own thing, the more effective and effortless the work was going to be, for both.

She did, however uncomfortable it was to give up any sense of control.

One hand cupped the right shoulder. The other positioned itself underneath the left breast.

First he isolated the diseased area to avoid energising cancerous cells, he explained.

She heard him breathe heavily several times, sensed his hands trembling a bit before he took them off her body. When he asked her to relax and keep breathing, she became aware how, involuntary, she'd tensed up and held her breath.

"Sorry", she whispered.

"Don't worry. You're doing great, Esther. It's no wonder you feel a bit uptight, lying here with a total stranger's hands all over your body. Just keep breathing and if there's anything I say or do, that you don't feel comfortable with, please let me know. You feeling safe is one of the most important ingredients of our time together."

"I'll do my best."

Her body tried to nestle into greater comfort, she fidgeted, breathed deeply and closed her eyes. His hands went to her feet, she saw, peeking through narrowly opened eyelids. Immediately she berated herself, for peeking was not doing her best, but how could she resist? It was all so new, so strange, so unfamiliar. Besides that, her life was depending on her surrendering like that patient he had described in his book. Also she now was putting her life into his hands. Hope. Trust. Unicorn.

Nothing happened when his hands moved from joint to joint and over certain energy points, like he had explained. Nothing much happened. His hands lingered, one over her heart, directly between her breasts and the other low down, between her calves. Still nothing happened.

"Try and picture your mother, Esther. See if you can make eye contact with her, take a couple of long deep breaths and exhale through your mouth."

She did. The other woman from the story had felt her mother being present in spirit in this very room, lying on this very bench. Was he trying to get her geared up for a similar meeting? She was prepared, willing and as ready as she'd ever be.

"Just breathe into your heart and try to switch off your mind as much as possible."

There was really no escaping his scrutinising perception. OK, back to the drawing board. First she took a quick in and out breath, then she did as he asked and looked at her mother during these final stages of her sickbed, lying still with the sunken eyes half shut in a tired exhaustion. Pale and pasty had been her face and her eyes sunk more hollow and deeper into their sockets by the day. The round and rosy cheeks had faded and a few thin strands of hair had lain plastered on her practically bald skull, the last remnants from a riches of hair, which had once been her mother's and father's pride and joy.

A tickle in her throat refused to be cleared. She coughed a few times and a few times more often and a few times more often and deeper. Initially she tried to put a hand in front of her mouth as the civilised thing to do.

He prevented her by simply taking the wrist and removing her hand. Somewhere in a hazy distance he uttered some inaudible explanation, praised and encouraged her to continue coughing.

As if she had a choice. From taking effort in the beginning, her coughing became effortless. Her body coughed incessantly all by itself and wretched and she heard the awful sounds she produced. I'm becoming uncivilised to the extreme, she thought cynically amidst the ordeal and less than a minute later, nauseousness could no longer be repressed either. Well, that was going to be embarrassing if she had to puke right there and then in front of this strange man. She felt a wave emerging and went to sit upright with a bolt.

"Do you need to throw up?"

"Maybe. I really don't want to, but ….."

Before she knew what happened, he briefly stepped away from her, returned with a plastic washing up basin and placed it between her lower legs.

"Just in case. Don't hold back. You've done that long enough. You've held back for decades. This is catching up time for you. By all means make use of it, Esther. Or, spit things out, if that's what you need."

Amidst all the internalised chaos externalising itself, she heard her name being mentioned. How comforting that sounded, how unfathomably comforting and a wave of sobs escaped. They didn't replace the retching, though but were added to the waves of release. Coughing, retching, sobbing and spitting happened all at once and for dear life she held on the rims of the washing up bowl.

In between handing her piles of tissues, one of his hand rested reassuringly on her back, somewhere behind her heart and one on her front, directly below the ribcage. The latter put a slight pressure on, as if he forced her to puke.

"Can't be a pleasant experience for him if I throw up." she thought and spat another chunk of phlegm into the basin. "Where for heaven's sake does it all come from?" she wondered during a lucid minute in between surfacing waves.

Once a next surge rolled through her upper body, thoughts vanished. Her body and its collapsing armour demanded one hundred percent concentration and there was absolutely nothing she could do about the procedure taking its own course. Tiredness crept in and made her even more defenceless. A wet rag had more body than she did and she no longer felt the strength to stay semi-vertical and she dropped backwards.

Still, his voice sounded in a far, far distance.

She didn't understand a single word, didn't have the energy to make an effort and let his messages be for what they were.

Yet again her body demanded her to pay full attention. It prickled all over, from the tips of her toes, to her fingertips, to her head. The sensation was similarish to what she had experienced in her fingertips early that morning after dreaming.

"Had the dream been a premonition?" her mind questioned.

Especially her lips felt strange and her chin started to tremble. Her shoulders ditto and they made her arms and hands shake uncontrollably. They waved, shocked, jerked back and forth and up and down up to the point that her wrists were bent spastically, whilst all fingers straightened, tightened and locked together. She tried to rectify them, worried about her own peculiar behaviour.

His voice sounded firmer, probably in order to try and get through to her.

"Allow, Esther, allow. It'll feel strange and possibly scary, but your reaction is very normal over here. I've seen it before, many times and much stronger. Later on I'll explain it to you. For now, just allow, allow yourself to liberate your body or for your body to liberate itself."

All sense of time faded. She lay on the couch, out of control with a strange man's hands gently resting on her shoulder joints and felt lost in time and space during the process of finding. Finding what exactly? Her pain? Her suppressed grief? Her cause of cancer? Her true self?

Gradually normal physical sensations returned to the wet rag and some sense of control came back, first in Esther's fingers and steadily moving throughout all other body parts. She felt a passive hand on her right shoulder and heard him speaking and his voice slowly becoming clearer until she was able to understand how he paid her a compliment and thanked her for her trust. He thanked her. My god, she ought to express gratitude to him lots and lots and lots, but she was still too dazed to respond sensibly. Yes, she'd love to drink some water and drinking a few sips helped to regain her voice. Not her usual soprano voice. Far from it. Janis Joplin's huskiness seemed more applicable.

"It's probably better not to enter any discussion or questions and answers today. Let's do that tomorrow, shall we? Otherwise you get caught up in your mind again and that can interfere with your healing rhythm for now. Is that OK?"

She nodded, delivering herself in his hands and following his advice to the letter. Esther slowly rose.

"Will you be all right to drive?"

"I will be. Don't worry."

"Great. Make sure you rest and drink plenty of water for the remainder of the day to support your body in releasing toxicity. And tomorrow we'll continue."

After these words he guided her out of the treatment room and to the front door, where she put her shoes back on.

She drove ever so slowly and carefully to her B&B. Back in her room she drank another big glass of water and collapsed in a heap, in a happy, contented heap, knowing that she had accomplished something extraordinary and convinced she could cure her cancer.

A comatosed two hours later, Esther awoke. A tremor vibrated throughout her entire body without resulting in the slightest physical movement. She lay still to locate it and was able to identify neither source nor direction. The trembling shifted from one area to the next in no specific rhythm or pattern. Her mind shifted alongside, with worry and wonder and trust taking turns.

Each of the three states of mind produced a different breath somehow and it was peculiar how she became aware of these fluctuations. Worry seemed as if it contracted the breath into shallowness, barely reaching the lungs. Wonder deepened her breathing slightly with a lightness not unlike the unicorn's vibration of her dreams, albeit not nearly that strong. Trust deepened or lowered it further still and made the breath heavier, as if causing it to reach way below her lungs and diaphragm, filling the whole of the abdominal regions, including the pelvis. Especially that area, the pelvis, felt as if on fire.

Why, she questioned, why would the pelvis feel aflame when the cancer had impacted the left breast? Why, if these sensations were a result of the treatment, why would not her breast be on fire if that's where healing would be expected to be concentrated physically? And so, questions kept surfacing. Esther wrote them down and instead of the list of questions reducing after one session, it lengthened. Was that part of her adding her bit to the healing process, was that her preparatory work, as he had put it? Then a next question, not to be forgotten, demanded to be written down. This one she wrote down with a smile on her face: "Is extreme appetite normal afterwards?"

Her stomach grumbled as if it hadn't been fed for weeks. Before she ventured into town, she went to the toilet and the odour of the urine made her nose wrinkle. She downed another glass of water, her third. Hadn't he written about something similar? Yet another thing to ask, although, would she feel courageous enough to ask something that private and embarrassing?

The idea crossed her mind to drive to the nearby coastal village and find a seaside restaurant for the catch of the day, but she decided against it. A leaden tiredness made every movement feel wearily heavy. Maybe it was advisable not to drive too far and leave the coastal outing for another day when she'd be left more energised, she concluded and headed for the town's High Street.

The choice of restaurants was limited. Esther had hoped for a sunny terrace, but found none. The café where she ended up, served a reasonable lasagne and she ate the lot. Fixated on her food, barely a thought crossed her mind. Even the excellently bitter espresso as desert didn't prevent her from yawning and almost drifting off to sleep there and then. Fixated on not yawning too openly and wide mouthed in public, thoughts stayed away once more or was drowsiness lazying the brain?

She paid, returned to her B&B where the door was never locked apparently and fell asleep, instantly, again. It was mid afternoon.

A full bladder called her awake, which was no wonder, after so many glasses of water. When she looked at her mobile, she was stunned: 1.18 a.m. and still faint daylight shone through the curtains.

Had she travelled this far north, that darkness was non-existent around midsummer? She opened the curtains enough to see the wide sky in a haze of velvety orange, pink and purple scattered clouds. Was dusk falling after a predominantly sunny day or did dawn already promise the next one, she questioned. Which was which at this time of night?

Aware that she kept travelling from one amazement to the next, she went and lay down on her back.

How did people catch enough sleep, when it never got dark? Well, she had slept and counted nine full hours of it. Nine hours of solid sleep and that after already two hours during the afternoon. She really had landed herself in a time warp.

Not just a time warp actually, because each experience was unusual and new. Had she first needed to enter a totally different environment in order to heal, as if her normal daily life needed to be left behind to facilitate a cure?

"Do I need to leave my normal daily life behind temporarily or for good?", Esther puzzled and her earlier emotional and unexpected reaction to the word "belonging" sprang to mind. Was this it? Did she belong here, in this rural part of the world so far up north? She'd be utterly flabbergasted if that proved to be the case or, even more astonishing and unbelievable to even contemplate, did part of her (all of her, she found too nonsensical to comprehend) belong to him, the healer? No way, she protested, he was at least twenty years her senior and not at all her type. She couldn't imagine that to be the underlying, subconscious reason for her reaction to "belonging". That was way too weird to even contemplate, argued her rational mind. Besides that, she hadn't even met him yet on the way from the airport, when tears had stopped her in her tracks and had forced her to park the car. But, what about spontaneous premonitions? He had explained her tingling fingers early that morning to possibly be a sign of some sort of inner preparation. In a sense she could interpret these physical sensations as another kind of premonition and one which had turned into reality, because only hours later her whole body had followed suit and tingled, in the process falling apart at the seams in its entirety.

Picturing her body falling apart at the seams in the literal sense of the word, made her smile. Looking back, it had actually felt exactly like that. Falling apart ought to take courage and the guts to surrender, but this kind of falling apart hadn't. Something had not given her a choice and had taken over before she had been able to keep herself in check.

Falling apart at the seams had a similar connotation to opening up, folding away outer layers to reveal the inner and that, she had done, doubtlessly and he had paid her compliments for daring to do so.

Would others have dared to surrender and fall apart? Gwyneth? Dominique? Charlie? Her father? She could envisage none of them in her position, but then, if roles had been reversed, they might well have thought the same of herself. Besides that, had any of them stored such pain and grief and anger during their lives? Her father did, unquestionably so with all his grief glossed over within a few months by Charlie's appearance. The fact that he had buried his grief, had become painfully apparent in hospital a few months earlier.

Would he get cancer as a result? With knowing so much more now, did she have the responsibility to inform him, particularly when her cancer was going to be cured during this trip?

That thought took Esther by surprise, even though it poured forth from her own brain. Was that what she really thought, that her secondary cancer could be cured? It was all too fantastic and fanciful to consider and still …..? Hope had resurfaced after just the one session and three more lay ahead. What a difference today's treatment was in comparison to chemotherapy. Horrified she looked back at what a state she'd been in with three chemo-therapy treatments behind her and her dreading the last three. This time she didn't dread the sessions, more the opposite. The prospect filled her with excitement.

Gradually Esther's thoughts slowed down and sleep encapsulated the preoccupied mind. The smile persisted.
CHAPTER 20

The extreme tiredness. The excessive yawning. The insatiable appetite. The falling apart at the seams. Esther's father's chances of attracting cancer. Questions on tap, one after the other, were pouring out of her at the beginning of the second meeting.

He didn't bat an eyelid, explained and interpreted her entire account as a sign, that her physique absorbed the healing well and when he asked about possible night sweats, smelly urine or diarrhoea, she didn't feel at all embarrassed to admit to the second.

Finally she told of her spontaneous notion that she was capable of being healed. Was that idea pure madness stemming from her wishful thinking or might it contain a smidgen of truth after all?

"Well, we definitely made a brilliant start, Esther. Everything you report is positive. At the same time, I don't want to give you too much hope. Let's simply keep doing our best, like we did yesterday and then see where we end up by Friday, shall we? Also, for now, try not to expect a repeat of yesterday. The first session is often the most dramatic one."

With that, she lay down and closed her eyes. The temptation to peek no longer came to the fore.

Once he had positioned himself back at her feet, he said:

"You definitely did a great job yesterday. No doubt about that. The energy flow has increased tremendously throughout your entire system. That means, we can now start to work directly on your cancer and I'll restructure your left breast on all seven levels of its aura. It helps, that you've read up on the theoretical bits before you arrived here. It saves me from explaining every single detail."

For a split second she tried to recall what she had read, failed to remember any details and thought:

"What the heck. Relax. Surrender. Hope. Trust. Unicorn."

For quite some time she felt his hands moving around her breast without the slightest touch. All the while she breathed deeply and slowly, like he prompted her to do, but nothing in particular happened.

He mumbled inaudibly, whilst his breath quickened every now and then.

It felt as if electric currents pierced her breast and as if something deep, deep inside her shifted. That something

146

moved from the inside outwards and disappeared altogether. It felt like a chunk, a clump of whatever stuff and unidentifiably dark, if not entirely black. Then, weirder still, she received an impression of strings. As if deep inside her breast a ball of yarn was unwinding, again black.

His breath became erratic, whilst the ball kept unwinding, unwinding, unwinding, until there was no ball left and his breath calmed down. He took a chair and sat down next to her with both hands adjacent to her breast. His breathing returned to its previous speed and intensified further still. One hand trembled ever so slightly.

Momentarily Esther tensed up when it felt as if his fingers entered her breast. These same fingers seemed to fold around a hard clump. Was that her actual tumour? The fingers held on tightly and other fingers moved around the clump as if cutting it free from its surroundings. How many fingers were involved, she couldn't guess. Dozens, it seemed. Prickling, tingling, electric shocks, tremors and a series of unidentifiable sensations heated her breast. Esther experienced sensations like being on fire, but then a pain free burning. Her left arm began to move, to wave, to lift up and down all by itself, to bend and straighten at both her elbow and her wrist until a seemingly high voltage current burst free from her breast, shot straight through her shoulder and arm and out of her fingertips. They regained that now familiar electrified feeling, with one difference. In addition, she sensed a glow or a heat building up. Esther's whole left hand side was aflame.

"Great." he muttered and pushed the chair back. He took a few deep, long breaths as if to give himself a breather. One hand came to rest on her shoulder and his other hand's whereabouts she was unaware of. Once again his breath went berserk, but differently, very fast and shallow this time.

A shower of light penetrated her left breast, armpit and arm. The light shone in a purity she had never imagined possible and definitely never experienced before. Golden, silvery, pearly, the light moved down from somewhere above and filled every cell with its shininess. Once the shininess enveloped and bathed her whole body, a weightlessness came over her as if no body existed, as if she was being liberated from all physical burdens and as if she existed of light, only light.

The unicorn appeared in her field of vision as if to make her aware that they had now reached a similar brightness and transparency.

Esther's tears flowed abundantly out of pure joy and bliss. The light bath appeared to lift anything out of her that still carried weight. She floated into an exquisite eternity and lay there, supine and unaware of surroundings until part of her no longer registered his hands or breath. She opened her eyes, didn't notice him next to the couch and directed her eyes to his chair.

He sat there and smiled silently.

"Do you want me to get up?"

"Yeah, but slowly. A lot has happened, Esther. If you move too fast, you may get dizzy. Would you like some water?"

She did and pushed herself into a sitting position, downed the first glass and sipped the second.

"That's one thing I'm learning here: to drink water in massive quantities."

"Hopefully you're learning other things besides?"

"Gosh yes, but please, don't ask me to recall any right now. My head is not screwed on properly or maybe it is now, where as it wasn't before. Who knows?"

"Well put. Who knows which way your head needs to be screwed on or which way anybody's head needs to be screwed on? In my opinion, your head is screwed on far better than that of most people, Esther. You're in the process of getting your priorities right, aren't you?"

"Do you think so? All I want, is to get better."

"Often it takes a different approach to life in order to achieve that and heal the root of the disease. My sense is, that you wont return to your previous life with the same attitude, or do you intend to?"

"I shall need to think about that one."

"Fair enough. Did you feel anything particular during our session just now?"

"You bet."

Esther recalled in great detail all she remembered and when she described the light bath, tears welled up.

"You really do show a great perception, Esther. Not everybody feels the work in such detail. Excellent, because it's OK for me to tell you my perception. However, it's much more encouraging if you experience it consciously yourself. Let's carry on tomorrow, shall we? Most likely you will still feel tired later today, but not as wiped out as yesterday. The first session normally has in this respect the biggest impact. Tomorrow, if you wish, we can answer lots of your questions, because I realise, that I've hardly given you any opportunity to do so."

Tjitze de Jong

CHAPTER TWENTY

"Before we get to your round of questions, Esther, how have you been these last twenty four hours?"

She told him how she, as on the previous day, had returned to her B&B to rest, but sleep hadn't come this time. Instead, a restlessness had forced her to get up. Initially she'd resisted, but the impulse had persisted and she'd succumbed, had driven to the seaside and had sat on the endless beach with waves rolling pebbles back and forth into an impeccable smoothness. She'd stuffed her pockets of stones, mesmerised by the immense variety of colours and patterns and wonderment had made her totally loose track of time.

Wonderment about the expanse of sea and sand and stones, converging into a wideness where no people seemed to have impacted on the natural abundance and where timelessness ruled.

Wonderment about the sessions and their revelations of how

deeply she had buried her emotions and how they had influenced her health and body negatively by repressing her joi de vivre.

Wonderment that she was able to be healed, despite that dreaded diagnosis of secondary cancer.

Wonderment about his remarks, that she, most likely, wouldn't return to her previous way of life and that she'd need to take a different approach to life altogether. What was that going to imply? Which consequences were going to follow and how far reaching might these turn out to be? Did she have to quit her job after all those years, for example?

Wonderment whether he'd also been able to cure her mother all those years ago?

Wonderment if cancer was festering inside her father's body without him being aware of it, like she hadn't had the foggiest of cancer festering before the actual diagnosis. Also he carried lots of suppressed emotions around with him and lived in a state of continuous denial.

Wonderment about her voice and whether it might ever return to a regular pitch perfect soprano?

"And so," Esther concluded, smiling, "I'd love you to answer all of these questions or comment on all of the above and then your answers will, no doubt, raise another thousand and one new questions. Strange as it sounds to my own ears, I feel as if I am not in the slightest in need of answers and explanations. Life has brought me here and cancer has. The cancer has brought me to a much deeper understanding of myself, of health, of illness and of my own role in it all. Gosh, how can I get my head around it all, the old me is saying. Try not to get my head around it all and trust the unicorn, the new me is saying. Truly, I can not believe that this mixture of thoughts is my own."

"The time was or is right, Esther, for you to undergo such a transformation. Playing the game with that card of "trust", picturing the unicorn, as your guardian angel was a first step. From then on, often unbeknown to yourself, you have dared to step forward, faced the hurdle of cancer and have overcome that, hopefully. All I can say is: well done, well done."

They sat in silence for a couple of minutes within an atmosphere of budding potential, permeating the room and when he asked, whether she'd like to lie down, she did and no further word was spoken.

Until he positioned himself again at her feet, held them gently and said: "As I stated before, Esther, I am not a medical doctor and therefore I am unable to diagnose you. Still, I no longer sense cancer in your breast. I do not say this lightly, because I don't want to get your hopes up, but I can not deny what my sense is."

The voice sounded monotonous and almost trance-like. Each syllable stretched a touch longer than was strictly necessary.

Tears were her sole reply.

"Breathe, Esther, breathe light. Breathe light into your breast, into your lymphatic system. Breathe light into every cell of your body. Fill yourself with light, light, light, ever more light. You can never overdose on light. Breathe, breathe in freedom of body, mind and spirit. Breathe, to celebrate your life. Breathe, to celebrate you're alive."

Once the session had finished, all she could report, was, how her body had been flooded by light. From no source in particular, light had streamed through every nook and cranny and in every direction and from every direction conceivable. To be more precise, it hadn't streamed or flooded, but all of a sudden her insides as well as her skin had lit up like a Christmas tree. Childhood sparkles sprang to mind, like she, scared of the sparks and fascinated by them, had held at a safe distance in a tight fisted grip, both scared and in awe. Now she herself had turned into such a sparkle without the slightest fear, but in total and utter awe.

There'd been trembling, this time more of a high pitched vibration as an all over body experience. Strange, involuntary movements, like the ones occurring in session one and two, had been absent. There'd simply been that vibration, unidentifiable, yet undeniably present.

However unfamiliar the impressions were, they'd oozed comfort as if she'd been held, enveloped and embraced by a force or a forcefield way bigger and more powerful than herself, or any human being for that matter.

At some stage during the session, Esther's mind had questioned, whether this was what it was like when being high or stoned. Curiosity had tempted her as teenager, especially when friends at school experimented secretly and had offered her a joint on one occasion. She had refused, obviously, because fear had maintained the upper hand and in particular the fear of becoming addicted, the fear of sleaziness and improperness, the fear of touching a cigarette with her lips, where strange lips had left their wet mark into the soggy paper. Then and there, she'd been proud of her discipline, although, within the hour and ever since, she had regretted her refusal. By refusing the joint, Esther had also refused a rebellious act and had refused a step towards adulthood, towards independence and towards an individual identity. By refusing the joint, she had obeyed the prim and proper image of her family and how they had expected her to follow in their footsteps. Clearly, that attitude had not allowed her parents to live a life of longevity, together, happily and contented.

Addiction to her present kind of high during a so-called light bath could definitely do no harm, her mind concluded and silenced in sweet surrender.

The light continued to beam within, also after the guy withdrew. The radiation simply refused to withdraw together with him and she basked in its bliss, unwilling to move.

"Can I stay here for the rest of the day?"

"We'd get in conflict with the next client. If you'd been the last one of the day, it would have been fine. You look just great, Esther."

"I feel it. Gosh, I never experienced anything like it. Is this what it's like to be high, stoned?"

"Not dissimilar. This is healthier and cheaper in the long run, because you can invoke these frequencies yourself."

"Can I?"

"Sure, You don't need me or anybody else for that. If you wish, I can teach you tomorrow. Tomorrow we'll have a very different type of healing as our final one. More like consolidation of what's been happening during the first three sessions to help your body, mind and spirit to integrate and digest all that has been stirred up and everything you've released. In this way we create a stronger foundation for your new self to build upon, so to speak. Before we start, I can try and teach you how to embody this inner light effortlessly, if you like."

"Yes please. I'd love that. You think I can learn it easily?"

"Can't see why not. Your intention is strong and positive, as is your perception. But, I'm sorry, I will need to throw you out now. The next client will be here in about fifteen minutes."

Esther's body floated into the car. The car floated to the coastal village. She floated through the shop for a bottle of water and then settled on her beach spot.

Tourists and locals alike were surfing, sailing, swimming and the overall atmosphere was festive, relaxed, befitting her mood. She wanted to be filled by the festivities around her and simultaneously fill all people on the beach with her light in order to create and take part in a seaside festival of light with her inner light joining sun beams playing on the sparkling waves. All light sources she wished to see merging into one for all to enjoy, for all to benefit from.

Esther drank copious amounts of water and when she needed the toilet, she stripped off into her underwear and went into sea, shivered in the chilly waters and felt invigorated for it. Back on dry land, sun and wind dried her.

She pondered about what was happening to her. Never in the world would she contemplate doing a thing like that and there she sat in soaked underwear after emptying her bladder in the sea. Nobody had noticed and nobody criticised her or warned her of some imminent danger. Going in the sea to pee had sprouted forth totally out of her own free will, out of spontaneity. Another sign of liberation if ever there was one and from now onwards all of her actions and decisions would be her own, solely her own and no one else's. No longer was she going to belong to other people and their fears or judgements or opinions and especially not their expectations of her. Indeed, especially not their expectations of her. From now on she belonged to no one.

Not to her father and most definitely not to Charlie. These two were allowed to live their lives as they pleased with their pretence or without it, with cancer festering or without cancer festering. It was up to them and their sense of self-respect to yes or no take responsibility.

Not to the choir, where none, during her illness, had lifted an administrative finger as far as she'd been informed. Esther promised herself to find another choir and in the meantime, that previous lot were forced to take responsibility themselves.

Not to the bank. She'd continue working there, but on her terms and after some sort of recognition of her loyalty, possibly in the form of some sort of promotion. If not, she'd leave, Esther promised herself.

Her wishes, her priorities counted in future and from now on she was going to belong to herself, just to herself. That thought made her mind stop in its tracks, whilst a shiver ran up and down her spine.

Belonged. Belonging. To belong.

That verb surfaced again. Initially it had brought tears to her eyes, decades ago, seemingly, although it had only been three days in actual reality. Unimaginable, three days ago only she had arrived here and not even that, counting in hours. Tears returned and her head shook in disbelief.

CHAPTER TWENTY ONE

According to him, the last treatment was going to be a very
different kind of session in order to support integration of the
first three treatments. How, she puzzled. What did she still
need to integrate, for it felt as if the third treatment had already
cemented total healing. Cemented through a light bath,
however contradictory these terms sounded within the one
sentence. The intense vibrations had gradually eased during
the day, but when Esther had gone to bed and lain on her back
to check how her body fared, some of these light sensations
had persisted, again mainly in her pelvis funnily enough,
which had brought her to yet another question to ask if time or
priorities allowed.

Despite all the questions she'd been wanting to have
answered initially, she had only asked the occasional one in
comparison. Questioning felt like sidetracking or a distraction
from the actual work she'd come for. Esther couldn't imagine

that knowing more facts would have contributed to the overall healing and she'd done it. She'd done it without knowing so many details. Well, that's at least what he had reported, but then again, could he be believed? Esther saw no reason why she couldn't believe him, because, what had he said at some point? Hadn't it been something along the lines of him being able to say whatever he wanted, but her own body gave the most accurate information?

If, in his book, he had described healing as a mythological journey, replacing darkness with light, then Esther could draw no other conclusion, than that the incredible vibrations in and throughout her whole body were positive signs and encouraging in the extreme. She'd progressed in leaps and bounds without a single hint of a doubt and her body told her so, as did her mind, which had been overly cynical in the past. Also he had said how she'd progressed and his remark confirmed her own perception. Even at the beginning of the third session he had observed her to be cancer free according to his observation and that amazing light bath had come on top of that.

Her mind kept making twists and turns, back and forth between doubt and trust, however, trust gained the upper hand for the first time in months and that fact alone seemed miraculous.

The next morning, on reporting, he merely smiled and, yet again, paid her a compliment, emphasising her timing, her capacity to trust and her willingness to surrender.

She decided to limit her questions to one only, the burning one and by far the most significant and all-encompassing one.

"You really think I've healed?"

"Dear, dear Esther, I'd love to reply in the positive, but I can never say for sure. My observations are not often wrong. If you want to know the truth, and naturally you do, I recommend you to visit your GP and request a scan as soon as possible. That'll provide you with the proof you request and hopefully we can give your medical staff a surprise."

Filled with anticipation she lay down, only partly comforted by his reply. Her curiosity remained unanswered and it left a bit of a bitter sweet taste, being unable to get the satisfaction she longed for with all her heart and soul. A lot of waiting had been involved these foregone months and that wait continued and might well take ages. Again, as a first step, she needed to book an appointment with her doctor, who then had to request a scan. Most likely a fortnight of waiting would be the least to expect and on top of that came another fortnight before scan results were due normally. Forced to wait close to a month altogether sounded like eternity. She had no choice in the matter other than ring her health centre today to speed things up. Once Esther made the decision, her mind quietened down and she was ready for whatever.

No inner light appeared. Nor were there these fluctuations in breathing from either him or from herself. Nor did she experience the variety of prickling and tingling and other vibrations. Nor was there that trembling from his hands or fingers reaching inside her breast and no removal of anything in particular. Quietude reigned, except for his hands changing position occasionally.

Instead of weightlessness, she underwent the exact opposite. Slowly, ever so slowly, a leaden heaviness took hold of her. Whatever she'd come to expect during this final healing, definitely not to gain pounds in weight. Whereas previously her body had moved unexpectedly in unprecedented ways, it now lay motionless, pinned down almost, unable to move a pinky. Whereas the excessive movements had been alarming in the beginning, today's total inactivity also rang alarm bells, especially due to the fact, that she felt nothing else, absolutely nothing else, whilst her perception had been branded as very accurate by him. She perceived nothing else but this excessive weight gain. What was happening to her now again? Prior to her first healing, he had warned of involuntary movements, emotional outbursts and the like, but he'd never mentioned a word of warning about the possibility of being weighted down in the extreme and there was nothing she could do about it, paralysed as she'd become. This final healing turned into yet another act of surrendering to faith and trust. In her mind's eye, she pictured the first unicorn vision and for some reason prompted herself to concentrate on the creature.

It was as shiny as ever and moved towards Esther in slow motion until it positioned itself immediately opposite her and bent its head as if bowing to her, as if honouring her. It proved a perfectly calculated move, for it stood at precisely the right distance for the tip of the horn to touch her front ever so delicately. Again in slow motion, the tip drew a line from the centre of her forehead, over her nose, lips and chin, over the soft section of her throat and down her breastbone, over abdomen and pelvis and carried on in between her legs without touching, until the unicorn knelt and the horn touched the earth in the middle between her feet.

The picture of the angel card in the game had been reversed. The angel had been on bended knee in front of the unicorn, offering herself or her services in trust. Now, in reversed roles, the unicorn appeared to pay homage to her.

No sooner did that idea surface, then a bolt shot straight through her and for a split second a massive shudder rocked all quietude. After calming down, she still felt the same heaviness. However, in addition, Esther noticed a line, more accurately, a solid cast iron rod penetrating from top to bottom through the very centre of her body and beyond, way beyond. The line reached higher than her crown, way higher. The line reached lower than the earth between her feet, way lower. An incredible strength rushed throughout her physique and she felt powerful beyond measure. All different sections of her body attached themselves directly to that central line somehow. Stronger than ever before, her body felt to be her own, totally and utterly her own, belonging to her. The strength knew no rigidity, despite the initial association with an iron rod and each joint contained some sort of fluidity without actual motion.

Out of the blue, his breath quickened and that light returned. The very same vibration as during the third session enveloped and penetrated her once more. A similar exquisiteness became palpable again, together with an ecstasy of a similar magnitude and Esther inhaled powerfully to assure the light reached all of her. A breath of relief followed, when she tried to move her pinky and succeeded. The heaviness had vanished. "Ridiculous actually," she thought, "how important the movement of a pinky can be." and settled down to enjoy her final minutes on the couch and make the most of it.

He sat down after a few minutes as a sign of completion.

Esther lay and bathed in light, a bright light with these all-penetrating particles of light like during the third session. The difference was subtle with her physical body feeling more solid. Each light particle felt as if it grew roots into every cell of her physique, as if light and matter congealed inside her very body.

The actual healing had lasted less than half an hour. Talking about a time warp.

Sitting upright, she asked what that had been all about.

"Basically, a solidifying of the first three treatments", he said, "It aims to support your system physically as well as energetically in order to absorb more fully, more consciously all it has released and received these last three days, Esther. It helps the positive effects of our work to settle stronger, to increase its healing impact and it ought to increase your overall immune system. What I recommend to you, is to take it easy over the forthcoming weeks if your schedule allows for that."

"It does", she said and filled him in on the decisions she'd made regarding her father and Charlie, regarding her work and choir and that from now on her own priorities would come in first place.

"You're learning well, Esther. In that respect you've been a joy to work with. If you have any questions or when you struggle with keeping on track, don't hesitate to send me an e-mail. And please, do let me know your scan results."

"Oh, I shall. Can I ask you a final question, though?"

"Sure."

"That one woman, client, in your book, had lost her mother to cancer, like myself. Her mother was predominantly present in spirit during your work with her and their contact appeared to contribute strongly to her healing process. Did my mother not help to cure me? Was she never present?"

"Not as far as I'm aware."

"Why not? Or is that a silly question. Does that mean, that my contact with my mother is not important? Or has it become distorted or something?"

"Good question, Esther.", he said, "No, as far as I'm aware, there's nothing amiss with the relationship between you and your mother. For the other client that specific relationship seemed extremely significant to support her cure. Why? Most likely due to unfinished business on a personal level. It's often essential to iron out such issues in order for the souls, the spirits to be able to move on separately. For some reason, which I can't explain, that particular dynamic seemed irrelevant to your healing. You had the unicorn and that's pretty awesome and unique. I've never come across that phenomenon before."

"Really? I thought all these wacky things were normal for you."

"In a way, yes, And then again not at all. I've learned to always expect the unexpected, because everybody is so uniquely unique."

"Yeah, guess so.....Oops, here comes the next question. Have you got time?"

"Another five minutes will be OK."

"What caused my cancer?"

"That's multi-faceted, Esther. Experiencing your mother's illness at close hand and your grief around it, will definitely have been a major factor. Also, you not living freely from your own power, your own centre, will doubtlessly have contributed, but you are aware of that now and are doing remarkably well on this front. Then, try to eat less sugar or avoid it altogether, because cancerous cells feed on sugar. And try not to eat any microwaved and ready made meals. Eat lots of greens and start to grow your own sprouts from lentils, alfalfa seeds, mung beans, chickpeas, etc. You can google all necessary information and use the method you find easiest. Also, do you have an electric alarm clock?"

"Yes, I do."

"Do away with it. During the daytime your body is being bombarded by electrical currents with a frequency lower than that of our human bodies, because of all the electric equipment we're surrounded by. There's not really any avoidance possible there, especially when you live in a city. Your aura can restore itself during the night if your bedroom is free from electrical equipment. As I said earlier, a healthy and strong aura functions as a buffer zone and is essential for a strong immune system. Therefore, always switch off everything and leave nothing on standby. The same counts for wifi. Just from now on, use a cable, a simple so-called old fashioned cable."

"Gosh, if what you say is true, it's no wonder cancer is on the increase."

"Well, I'm not telling porky pies. You can research all these topics easily. One last thing. Do you always have your mobile switched on?"

"Yes."

"How and where do your carry it?"

"In my handbag."

"How do you carry your handbag?"

"Over my left shoulder."

"Thought as much. That means, Esther, day after day radiation from your mobile depletes your aura around that part of your body: your left breast and lymph nodes. There you have one of the main reasons why breast cancer is increasing rapidly among women and with men it's testicular cancer, for men mostly carry their mobile in their pocket."

"Gosh, I've read about some of this, also in your book, but never took it seriously. I'm learning so much."

"That's the one of the main reasons you've come here. And now I need to throw you out again and prepare for the next client."

Esther got up. On the way out, she thanked him profusely and they said their goodbyes.

CHAPTER TWENTY TWO

Looking forward to the consultation, she waited eagerly for her name to appear on the notice board and didn't dare miss it this time. On the contrary, before the red flashing letters of her name had completed scrolling from right to left over the screen, she arrived at the indicated door and knocked, louder than strictly necessary. Was it a sign of bravery or courage? Neither, because, why mention either bravery or courage when the eagerly awaited results would be a foregone conclusion? Esther's mind reduced the visit to a mere formality and saw the consultation as secure as collecting a pregnancy test without sex beforehand, she thought, inwardly smiling.

Still, her heart beat in her throat, whilst waiting for the summons. It felt that formal.

The wait for a scan had been shorter than anticipated, largely because she'd rung the medical centre within the hour of completing the series of treatments up north. Her return flight had been scheduled for later that day and early next morning she'd managed to book an appointment.

The GP had briefly scanned her file in her presence and

asked, whilst reading, what he could do for her. He had addressed her with the usual anonymous Ms.

"My name is Esther. Can you, please, from now on call me by my first name: Esther?"

"If you insist."

"I do and I'd like you to make a note of it on the outside of the folder, so yourself and your colleagues will know in future."

He'd obeyed without commenting and repeated his question, emphasising the pronunciation of her name. Had he accentuated her name to make sure she noticed or was there a hidden hint of ridicule?

Anyway, she'd managed to persuade him to schedule a scan the following week and when he had asked the reason behind her request, she didn't give anything away about her meddling in alternative therapies. His reaction would most likely have been cynical and she hadn't felt like defending her decision, but had merely said that it would help her make up her mind which next steps to take, once she'd know the exact, present state of affairs. Esther had played it safe and achieved her aim.

In the meantime, when opening the door of the consultation room, her heart beat in her throat.

Charlie especially, but also her father, had ridiculed her decision to book flights and sessions in order to undergo some voodoo sort of wizardry she'd only read a thin and unscientific book about. Any charlatan could have written it to coax desperate women into his money grabbing claws, had been Charlie's opinion.

Had she made any independent enquiries about his reputation? And when her reply was negative: had she even spoken to him? And when her reply was negative: how for heaven's sake, could she be so stupid to put her trust in such an unknown quantity and spend all that money?

Initially, the latter had been her father's sole contribution, referring to the financial side of her venture, obviously. What else could it have been, but after several minutes, his tongue had gained in sharpness, accusing both her and her mother, his late wife. Because, he had definitely not raised her to squander ridiculous amounts of money so naively. She didn't get her ridiculous spend-drift from him, as long as she'd realise that for a fact. Did she think, he hadn't explored alternative ways in order to keep his wife, her mother, alive and wouldn't he have done his utmost to save his wife's life, her mother's life and invested time and money if he would really be of the opinion that such charlatanism would result in the slightest chance of a positive outcome?

To each of the three components of his question, if it could be called that, of his interrogation to be more precise, she had wished to stand up and scream into his face: "No" and "No" twice and "No" thrice and stamp her foot real forcefully to get her point across. Courage had failed her, then. It would no longer have failed her after her northern adventure. The opportunity to make up for lost ground didn't materialise during Esther's next visit for the simple reason that there'd been no need for it any more.

On opening the front door for her, Charlie had said, spontaneously: "You look different."

Stepdaughter had been wearing neither a wig or a headscarf and her skull was covered in the downy fur, typical of chemo patients. Both her father and Charlie didn't like her to wear nothing on her naked head. They found it too confrontational, they'd said matter of factly, once no more tufts had been left to fall out.

Esther had waited with her reply until she'd seated herself in the living room, in the presence of, also, her father.

"I feel different." she said calmly. "Very different."

"Well, all I can say, you look it. How was it?"

"Awesome."

"Tell us more. Don't keep us in suspense. We want to know every single detail, don't we?"

The last question had been directed to her partner, who remained stoically silent.

"There really isn't much to tell. It was awesome."

"You must be able to give some further background information. What did he do? Did you cry?"

"Everything I can say about it, will sound over the top, far fetched and pulled grossly out of context. Me telling you details will make no sense. You need to experience it in order to believe it. The entire experience was awesome, believe you me."

Charlie had kept fishing and Esther had kept avoiding. She'd wanted it to remain her experience and hers only and for those experiences and memories not to be influenced, most likely soured, by the scepticism of other people.

Until her father, with a cynical undertone, had asked that crucial question:

"Has he cured you?"

"I don't know. He can't diagnose me, because he's not a medical doctor, hence doesn't have that authority. By the end of the week I'll get a scan and then we shall know more."

"What good does that do? That chap rubbing his hands whilst cashing your fat cheque, but, in the end, he's unable to tell you whether he's cured you or not. I'd happily put my all of my money on it, that it has all been a total and utter waste of time and money. I would not put my hopes up, if I were you."

"Shall we put that in writing, dad? I'll happily go along with your offer. I feel cured and if you feel that's worth your fortune, great, then I'll gladly sign on the dotted line."

Senior looked perplexed for a split second, just long enough for Charlie to put in her penny's worth.

"Do you have that much faith in your chap?"

"I have faith in what I've experienced. Let's put it that way."

Esther had anticipated attacks and also, that persuading either of them would be out of the question. Her suspicion proved correct. Once that notion became clear, she changed the subject to safer topics as soon as possible and inquired about what the couple had been up to these last weeks.

Their flight to the Isle of Wight in his four seater plane had been a total and utter bore. The wedding of the son of one of his customers, who was due to take the helm of dad's business within the year, had been as tacky and cliché as they'd expected. The bride had suffered from nausea and migraine attacks, due, naturally, to theirs being a forced marriage. Both the groom and his father had been highly irritated, most likely after some dispute. All guests had done their utmost to ignore the family dynamics and inconveniences and had pretended jolliness.

With a few well placed remarks and questions, Esther had kept the rest of that day's conversation on an even keel and had sighed a sigh of relief once Charlie had closed the front door behind her.

One box had been ticked with two more to go.

One of these boxes had concerned the choir. It had only taken a couple of minutes to e-mail Gwyneth and Esther had worded her resignation diplomatically: she, under present circumstances, felt unable to continue all activities regarding the choir, the administrative duties as well as actual participation. She had asked Gwyneth to give her regards to all members.

The reply had been slow in arriving and had contained a polite 'thank you' and a stereotypical well wishing from the other choir members.

The second box had been ticked with only one more to go.

Esther had rung her bank. Dominique had been on a three week holiday and when she'd asked, whether he could please give her a call on his return, the message would be passed on. His three weeks leave were not finished yet.

The third box had been semi-ticked.

Many other boxes had been ticked, but they hadn't concerned verbal communication and diplomacy and had been less complicated to accomplish. One of the first boxes had been a tour through the flat, switching off all electrical stuff on standby. Her father would approve of that, no doubt, savings on the electricity bill as a bonus. Next, she'd rummaged through the fridge and the cupboards and had read labels of all food items. Most of it had ended up in the bin. She quickly discarded the thought of bringing the stuff to a food bank or a thrift shop. Why encourage other people to eat unhealthily? The same had happened with her alarm clock and the microwave.

As a result, Esther's first shopping list had contained very different items than normal, including an old fashioned, ticking alarm clock, a cable for her laptop and pulses and seeds for sprouting.

The word "sprouts" lost its association with Sunday roasts and Christmas dinners. These pulses were cool, tiny shoots appeared within two days. Filled with apprehension and excitement, she put one green lentil on her tongue. All hardness had vanished and it had become chewable, thus digestible and actually tasted OK. More importantly, it felt alive, healthy and almost clean in her mouth. On the third day, she'd prepared a big salad with peppers, avocado, red onions, plenty of olive oil, sardines and Esther had overdosed on sprouts.

All of these adventures had occurred weeks ago. Now, her heart beat in her throat once she sat opposite her GP, not any longer out of fear, but her entire being was filled with an excitable anticipation.

When she entered, he was about to open her file and was distracted by his own note of a few weeks earlier.

"Esther, indeed. I remember. What can I do for you?"

"I come for the scan results."

"Indeed, yes. Here they are."

The man in white shifted his attention from the paper file to the one on the computer screen and he downloaded the relevant photographs. He took a look, in a rather uninterested routine-like fashion, then studied the images more meticulously with his face closer to the screen. Then he looked in Esther's direction and back to the screen.

"Can I take a look myself?"

"Eh, well, yes obviously, but there is nothing much to see. At least no cancer. Unless I'm mistaken."

He mumbled barely audible in a rather confused manner, turned the screen somewhat towards his patient and stood up to switch off the fluorescent lights in order to improve the screen's display, after which he sat down again, brought up her previous scan and projected both pictures next to each other.

"See", he pointed pensively to a darker area in her breast's image, "this darkness indicates cancerous activity. No doubt about that. And here, in our last scan, that darkness seems to have vanished. But why and how?"

Unadulterated joy rushed with her involuntary quickened breath through her veins and arteries, through her nerves and all through her physique. Her skin crawled. The implications of the GP's message made her hair stand up, if she had had any, that was. She remained silent, otherwise it would become impossible to control herself, but inwardly she cried a million tears of joy and gratitude.

She'd done it.

Whatever else the doctor said, asked, tried to explain as possible reasons for the tumour to have dissolved without extra chemo or radiotherapy, she didn't hear the monologue. All she heard were her silent screams of victory. She mumbled a vague "thank you", whilst he still spoke and Esther left the consultation room.

A few minutes later she stood on that very same spot, the entrance, precisely there where the hospital campus changed into public pavement. That vey same spot, where the first tuft of hair had fallen out.

Esther looked over her shoulder to the ugly building before turning her head. Ahead of her lay freedom, a life without cancer, without further appointments, consultations, chemotherapy, scans and the eternal waiting rooms. The diary would remain empty of all illness related dates and times from now on.

Uninvited Guest, Unexpected Gifts

Two obligations still required to be fulfilled. At some point she wanted to visit the Maggie's Centre to tell them her amazing news. Amid all their surrounding suffering, these volunteers needed a positive boost in order to support them who supported so many. The organisation had ultimately opened the door to her healing journey, unbeknown to them. Secondly, she had to e-mail her healer up North. Combined, these two had given her her life back.

Once the decisions had been made, Esther took a deliberately giant step over the threshold and left her cancer episode where she wanted it, in the past, forever. Then, tears followed for real and she cared no longer what passers by thought of her.

She'd done it.

Made in the USA
Coppell, TX
09 November 2020

41052252R00095